Books by Tom Hoffman

*Paperback versions available online
at Amazon or Barnes & Noble*

THE TRANSLUCENT BOY

and the man who
walked to the moon

by Tom Hoffman

With lots of love for
Molly, Alex, Sophie, Oliver,
and Naomi

Table of Contents

For all the amazing
translucent kids out there
who spend their days
listening, reading,
and thinking.

"One who looks outside, dreams.
One who looks inside, awakens."

– *Carl Jung*

"Where you stumble and fall,
there you will find gold."

– *Joseph Campbell*

THE TRANSLUCENT BOY

and the man who walked to the moon

Chapter 1

Odo's Dream Vacation

Odo Whitley leaned back in his green and yellow striped canvas beach chair, gazing across the pristine white sandy beach, a pair of nearby palm trees swaying gently in the ocean breeze. A bright green bird with long yellow legs was racing along the shoreline, scouting the area for its next meal. It stopped, poking its long beak into the wet sand, triumphantly pulling out a wriggling bug.

"I'm glad I don't have a beak. It would be really annoying trying to drink from a glass. Unless you could use your beak like a straw. But that would make eating cookies problematic at best."

Odo's best friend, Sephie Crumb, was seated next to him, slowly turning the pages of a tattered old leather bound book.

"Trying to read, Odo Whitley."

Odo looked away, enjoying the warmth of the

summer sun, the smell of the salty sea air, the rhythmic sound of the waves rolling onto the shore. He studied the myriad of small islands dotting the blue green sea. This was a marvelous dream and he was fully conscious in it, fully aware that he was dreaming. He grinned at Sephie. "We have our own little island, how cool is that? This is a dream vacation. Get it, a *dream* vacation?"

"Got it. Kind of busy, Odo Whitley."

"Why are you reading when we're at the beach? We should go for a swim. It's a dream, so we won't get wet, and there's no creepy stuff like sharks or crabs or those crazy moray eels that bite you and don't let go. They're scary. And no weird stinging jellyfish. Nobody likes jellyfish except the peanut butter fish."

"Mm hmm."

Odo frowned at Sephie's tepid response to his hilarious play on words. "What are you reading?"

"What?"

"What are you reading that's so interesting?"

"It's an old handwritten journal about Antarctica. It's fascinating, full of adventure, mystery, and intrigue. I'm just getting to a good part. It's very exciting. It would make a great movie."

Odo snorted. "An old journal about ice and snow? How boring is that? Let's go swimming. Don't forget, no sharks here."

"What is it with you and sharks?" Sephie closed her book, turning to Odo. "Why is there a door behind you?"

Odo whipped around, eyeing the white wooden door hovering two inches above the sand. "Where did that come from?"

Sephie shrugged. "I'm guessing the same place the sand and the ocean and the sky came from?"

Odo studied the door curiously. "It's my bedroom door. It has the same chipped glass doorknob and the paint is scratched from when Watson the Cat was trying to get out of my room. That was the day he knocked my dad's work camera off the kitchen table. Remember how I had to take the camera to Beasley's Camera Shop to get it repaired and I found that old photo of –"

"Focus, Odo Whitley. You should check out that door. Dream doors are always important, very symbolic."

Odo shrugged, twisting the knob and pulling the door open. "It's my bedroom. That's not weird and symbolic."

He stepped into his room, the door closing behind him, stopping when he saw a glowing blue medallion resting on his pillow. "That looks valuable, the glowing stone could be a sapphire, and it's a big one." He picked up the medallion, examining it. "Interesting. Looks really old. Too bad you can't bring stuff back from your dreams. I'm going to give this to Sephie, she'll love it." He smiled, imagining the look of surprise and delight on her face when he presented the sparkling blue sapphire medallion to her.

Much to Odo's dismay, when he flung open his bedroom door he was not greeted by looks of surprise and delight, but by an immense pair of curved black claws attached to a fourteen-foot tall yellow and blue speckled lizard creature with piercing black eyes, its rank, putrid breath assailing his nostrils.

Before Odo could react, the monstrous reptile had yanked him from his bedroom, flinging him into the thick spiny undergrowth of a sweltering dank jungle, sharp thorns stabbing into his arm. He groaned, staggering to his feet, skittering back when the massive lizard creature turned, rose up on two legs and lunged toward him with a deafening roar.

Odo jumped back, dodging its snapping jaws, colliding with a spiny tree trunk, the sharp spikes jabbing painfully into his side. The creature slashed at him with a huge clawed leg, missing by inches. Odo gave a screech, stumbling wildly through the leafy undergrowth, the lizard beast only yards behind him. "Worst dream ever! Time to wake up!" He raced ahead, ducking under a low branch, glancing at his arm. "I'm bleeding where the thorns stabbed me! Why am I bleeding? I'm solid, not translucent! This is bad!"

Odo was translucent on Earth, but solid on other worlds. It was clear to him that he had unwittingly dimensionally shifted to another world, a very real one where it would be quite possible for him to meet a grisly demise between the powerful jaws of this ferocious rampaging monstrosity.

He raced down a narrow jungle trail, running and

jumping over a tangle of thick twisted roots, letting out a shriek of horror when an eight-inch long flying insect smacked into his chest. The hideous wriggling creature was clinging tenaciously to his shirt with its hooked claws, its jagged mandibles opening and closing inches from his neck. He pushed at it with his elbow, too afraid to touch the hideous arthropod with his fingers. "Aggh! Get off me! Get off!" There was a blur of blue green iridescent wings, the creature slapping against his face before it disappeared into the shadowy rainforest.

Odo scrambled wildly down the trail, glancing behind him every few seconds, his eyes on the reptilian behemoth. He ran for almost half a mile, dodging between trees to avoid the beast, stopping when the creature finally let out a roar and turned abruptly, disappearing into the dense jungle.

Odo hunched over, trying to catch his breath. This was not good. That thing could have chomped him to pieces. How was he supposed to get home? He pressed his hand to his chest, feeling for his homestone pendant, remembering he'd taken it off before he went to bed.

Odo had been born translucent, the result of highly advanced genetically engineered nanobots secretly given to his mother during her pregnancy by Wikerus Praevian and Mrs. Preke. They had been well aware of the distress it would cause Odo as a child, of the deep loneliness and sense of rejection he would feel, but they also knew that from the flames of such adversity a hero would arise, a hero who would ultimately save Wikerus' home planet of Fortisia.

Being translucent also brought with it the curious ability to shift from one world to another using a waystone. When Odo held an otherworldly waystone in his hands and aligned his deeper vibrations with it, he was transported to the world of the waystone's origin. To return home the process was repeated using a registered homestone, a gift from Wikerus Praevian and Mrs. Preke.

His best friend Sephie Crumb was half Fortisian, and also a proficient shifter. They both wore homestone amulets, their tickets back from the alien worlds they visited.

"I don't have my homestone, so I have to find another way back. Wait, I can go back through my bedroom door, back to the beach where Sephie is! I'll circle around, watching out for that crazy monster lizard. That insect that landed on my chest was so creepy. I think it touched my lips. I hope I didn't catch some weird insect disease." He rubbed his mouth vigorously with his shirt sleeve.

He turned abruptly when he heard a deep humming sound coming from above the trees. "Is that an insect? I hate giant insects! Spiders are the worst." He ducked down, startled by the sight of a thirty-foot long sparkling silver craft shooting past a hundred feet above the forest canopy. "No way! It's not a bug, it's high tech, definitely an antigravity ship, no wings, no jets, and no propellers."

Four more ships flashed past above him. "I should check this out. If this is a high tech world, there could be an interstellar transition station I can use to get back to Earth." He was remembering the first time he and Sephie had visited Girard Station and taken an interstellar transition cylinder to the distant world of Plindor, Mrs. Preke's home world. It was the first time they'd seen aliens, Girard Station packed with bustling crowds of alien travelers from a hundred different worlds. It was also the first time they'd seen Sinarians, the enigmatic faceless beings who floated above the ground when they walked.

He ran for another ten minutes, emerging from the jungle next to a wide pale blue roadway. He kneeled down, touching the smooth surface, studying it closely. "It's made of a synthetic material, but it's not plastic. It tingles, like it has an electromagnetic charge running through it."

Odo jumped back, hiding behind a spiky tree when he spotted a massive conglomeration of vehicles streaking down the roadway toward him. There were hundreds of them, all sizes and shapes. He watched as the cars shot past, unable to see the drivers. "Whoa, those guys are moving, at least a hundred miles an hour. They're not antigravity cars, but they're traveling six inches above the roadway. Maybe this is a maglev transport system, definitely high tech. It could be an antigrav roadway, not just maglev."

He whipped around when he heard a deafening crash,

the sounds of shattering glass and twisting metal filling the air. One of the vehicles had veered wildly across the roadway, colliding with two others, all three of them spinning off into the jungle, exploding in a flash of white light, a massive ball of green fire erupting from the wreckage. "No one is stopping to help. What's happening here? Where are they all going?"

He crept forward until he was only a few feet from the roadway, keeping low until he realized that no one was paying any attention to him. Another vehicle spun out and flew off the road, but this one didn't explode. The driver staggered out of the craft, running down the side of the road.

"It's a big lizard guy, an alien. They're trying to escape from something. Maybe a bunch of those monster reptiles are headed this way. I should follow the cars, see where they're going." He ran along next to the road, hundreds of the floating cars flashing past him, dozens of antigrav ships streaking by overhead. He ran on, following the stream of vehicles, stopping abruptly when he saw their final destination.

"The ships are all going through a transition portal inside that giant dome. They're coming from everywhere, all directions. I wonder what they're running from? It must be really bad if they're leaving this world through a portal."

The answer to Odo's question arrived in the form of a titanic thundering explosion over forty miles away. The ground shook violently, knocking him to his knees, the shining synthetic roadway bending and snapping into long twisted shards, dozens of vehicles careening into the jungle, massive roiling balls of green fire erupting, clouds of white smoke billowing up into the sky.

Odo staggered to his feet, looking behind him. The sky was filled with pitch black rolling clouds of ash, orange yellow molten lava spewing miles up into the sky. "It's a volcano!" He heard a second massive explosion, the jungle floor rising up ten feet, hurling Odo against a huge gnarled spiky tree trunk, a three-foot wide crack appearing in the ground. He scrambled desperately to get away from it, clawing at the jungle floor, the earth shaking violently.

"I hate earthquakes! I have to get out of here. I have to get to that blue portal!" He jumped up, only to have the ground jerk sideways, slamming him against a spiky tree trunk. He sank to the ground, stunned. When he looked up at the churning black volcanic clouds an indescribable fear rolled through him. Hundreds of flaming molten boulders were streaking down from the sky toward him. There was no escape. He closed his eyes, waiting for the end. The worst of it was that Sephie would never know what happened to him.

Chapter 2

Terrorsaurus

Odo's eyes opened to the comforting sight of his cozy bedroom, but he wasn't certain if the room was real or a vision.

"I'm not dead, so that's good news." He pinched his arm. "Ouch. Definitely not dead, and I don't think I'm dreaming." He examined his arm where the spiky trees had stabbed him and drawn blood. "Not a scratch, and I'm translucent again, so I'm back home for sure. All good news." He was more than pleased to be home, but still deeply puzzled by his terrifying nocturnal alien jungle adventure.

"I know the volcano world was real, not a dream, because my arm was bleeding and I was solid, not translucent. But if it was a real world, why wasn't I killed by the giant falling rocks? It's possible the Sinarians may have helped me, brought me back here. It wouldn't be the first time they've saved me from–"

"Odo! Breakfast!"

Odo jumped up, hollering, "I'm getting dressed!" He pulled his clothes on, grinning when he remembered it was Saturday and he was going to the movies with his friends Sephie, Silas, and Emmy, all members of the *Odd Squad*, their little band of four unlikely superheroes.

"This is going to be so much fun. Silas picked the movie, and I have plenty of money for tickets and popcorn." He jammed his hand into his pocket, letting out a yelp when something stabbed into his finger. "Ow!" He gingerly pulled out a two-inch long curved triangular shaped thorn.

"No way! This is from one of those weird stabby trees in the jungle. How did that get in my pocket? This is proof I was in a real world and not a dream world." He wrapped the thorn in a tissue, hiding it in his sock drawer. "This is a good clue, it will help us figure out what world I went to. I'll have to do some research to identify it, maybe show it to Silas. He knows a lot about that kind of stuff and his grandpa knows even more."

"Odo! Your breakfast is getting cold!"

Odo flung open his bedroom door and ran down the stairs. As he stepped into the kitchen he called out, "Odo Whitley is in the house! All hail King Odo!"

His mom laughed, his dad did not. "What's wrong with you? Why are you yelling?"

"So you'd know I was here?"

Albert gave Odo an annoyed look. "You're translucent, not invisible. Everyone knows that. Besides, you came charging down the stairs like a herd of rampaging elephants. I'm surprised the neighbors haven't called to complain about the noise." He gave a loud laugh, glancing over at Petunia.

Odo said, "If you think about it logically, the stairway is three feet wide, and a full grown elephant is about twelve or thirteen feet wide, and at least–"

Odo's mom saw the growing look of annoyance on Albert's face, interrupting Odo. "How many eggs would you like?"

"Two, please."

Petunia smiled as she set the plate down in front of Odo. "All I can say is, it's a good thing for all of us that chickens are oviparous."

A very awkward silence filled the room.

Odo said, "Did you say oviparous?"

"It means they lay eggs. Oviparous."

Albert said, "Everyone knows what oviparous means."

Odo knew Albert had not known what oviparous meant.

Petunia grinned. She had taken a literature class at Gardner College, but she hadn't told Albert about it, afraid he would think it was silly, a waste of time and money.

Odo had been born translucent because Albert and Petunia had misconstrued the warning label on a bottle of Petunia's perfume, a gift from Wikerus Praevian, neither one of them knowing what the word *translucent* meant. Albert had confused it with the word *transcendent*. Petunia still blamed herself for Odo's translucent condition, vowing to improve her vocabulary so she wouldn't make a mistake like that again.

Odo grinned. "Impressive vocabulary."

"It's just something I read in a book."

Albert muttered, "There's more to life than books. Books don't pay the bills, hard work pays the bills."

Petunia nodded. "Your father is right. He works hard and earns a good living. He's up for a big promotion, you know."

"Really? What is it?"

Albert said, "A senior manager position in the Golden CrunchCake Division. It's a big responsibility with a big pay raise."

"Do you think you'll get it?"

"I hope so. There are seven other people applying for the job, but I have more experience."

"What are you going to do with all the money?"

"I don't have the position yet, but if I do get it, I'm not buying you a fancy computer, if that's what you're thinking."

Odo did his best to look appropriately offended. "Computer? What? No, I was thinking maybe you and Mom could take a dream vacation somewhere warm and sunny, maybe a tropical island or something."

Petunia grinned. "Doesn't that sound lovely? Sitting

on the beach watching the waves roll in, sipping one of those drinks with the little umbrellas?"

Albert stood up. "I'm too busy for tropical vacations." He stopped, eyeing Petunia. "But maybe later, if I get the promotion. I've always wanted to visit a tropical island."

Odo jumped up when he heard a knock on the front door. "I think that's Sephie. We're going to the movies. The early shows are a lot cheaper."

Albert nodded. "A wise choice. Money doesn't grow on trees. Everyone knows that."

Odo grabbed his jacket, running down the hallway. He cracked the door open half an inch, peering out at Sephie. "What's the secret password?"

Sephie Crumb shoved the door open. "The secret password is *Odo Whitley needs a new brain*."

Odo laughed. "Are you ready for an incredible movie? It's supposed to be really good."

Sephie grimaced. "*Terrorsaurus*? Really? That's the best Silas could do? Why do you two always pick dreadful movies like that? I brought a book to read while you're watching your incredible movie."

"Is it an old handwritten journal about Antarctica?"

Sephie gave a start. "What did you say?"

"I asked if you were reading an old handwritten journal about Antarctica."

"Why would you ask that?"

"Because last night I dreamed we were sitting on a beach and you were reading an old journal about

16

Antarctica."

"And you were watching a bright green bird with yellow legs run across the sand."

Odo took a step back. "What? How did you know that?"

"I had the same dream, Odo Whitley. It was so real."

"No way. We had the same dream?"

"You went through your bedroom door and never came back. I waited for you, but I finally woke up."

"This is incredible. We were sharing a dream. That's amazing."

"Why didn't you come back to the beach? What happened to you?"

"You're not going to believe this, but when I opened my bedroom door again, a huge–"

"Hey, Odo! Hey, Sephie!"

Odo turned, spotting their friends Silas and Emmy walking toward them. He waved to them, calling out, "Greetings, Ghostwatcher and Dream Girl!"

Silas laughed. "Are you ready to see the best movie ever made?"

Emmy made a face. "Let's hope it's the shortest movie ever made."

Sephie laughed. "Good one."

The four best friends headed down Expergo Street toward the movie theater, Sephie whispering to Emmy, "I brought a book to read during the movie."

Odo turned toward them. "I heard that, and I

guarantee you won't be reading it once the movie starts."

"Did you bring money for popcorn and candy? It's your turn to pay, in case you forgot."

"I didn't forget, and I have plenty of money. I just got my monthly retainer from Serendipity Salvage. Five hundred big fat juicy green dollars."

Emmy said, "Did Wikerus Praevian say anything more to you about our trip to Percupio, about Charon the Ferryman and his new steamboat? Or about bringing Jacob back from the Land of the Dead?"

"He didn't say anything more, but Mrs. Preke said how happy she was that the Sinarians didn't take away your ability to fly. She sounded really proud of us."

Silas said, "Those Sinarians are so strange, you never know what they're thinking. It's weird how they don't have eyes or ears or a mouth and they float above the ground when they walk. Speaking of floating, we don't need to walk to the theater, Emmy can fly us there."

"Nice try, Ghostwatcher. No flying on Earth, that's the rule. If anyone saw me fly it would be the end of the Odd Squad. We'd be prisoners in some weird secret government facility."

Odo said, "Or if they found out about Sephie's crazy mind powers."

Sephie punched his arm. "I don't have crazy mind powers, Odo Whitley, I have the natural ability to see people's brainwaves."

"And make them see stuff that doesn't exist."

Silas added, "And implant false memories in them."

Odo gave a smirky grin. "Like I said, your crazy mind powers."

Silas said, "There's the theater. Let's go, I don't want to be late."

Sephie turned to Odo. "I want a large popcorn and two boxes of candy. One of the candies has to have caramel, and one has to have nuts, but they can't both have nuts or both have caramel. It's okay if one of them has nuts and caramel, but then the other one can't have either. We can share them, but you only get half of the ones with caramel."

Odo stared at her. "That's way too confusing. Just pick out whatever you want and I'll pay for it. I'll get my own candy." He rubbed his hands together. "This is going to be so fun."

Sephie laughed, grabbing his hand as they entered the theater.

Chapter 3

Harold

One hundred and thirty-three minutes later the four friends emerged from the theater into the bright afternoon sunlight, Emmy rubbing her eyes, giving a loud yawn.

"That was the longest movie in the history of the universe."

"I know, wasn't it incredible? A classic, to be sure."

Silas nodded. "So good. I could watch it again. Wasn't it cool how the giant prehistoric pterosaur shot radioactive beams out of its mouth?"

"It was clever how they called it a *Terrorsaurus* instead of *Pterosaurus*. That was a good play on words."

"Really clever."

Sephie groaned. "Seriously? You think that was clever?"

Odo ignored Sephie's comment. "It was cool when the Terrorsaurus exploded those buildings and melted the tanks and planes."

Sephie stopped short. "It was ridiculous, every minute

of it. First of all, there's no way a prehistoric pterosaur could be living high up in the Himalayas. Dinosaurs need warm weather to survive, not to mention an atmosphere with an elevated concentration of oxygen because of their size. And what would it eat up there? Snow? Not to mention the fact that it couldn't shoot radioactive beams from its mouth because the radiation would kill it. Use your brain, Odo Whitley."

Silas was about to mention that pterosaurs were flying reptiles, not dinosaurs, and many dinosaurs had indeed lived in frigid snow covered regions of the world, but he decided against it. It would be way more fun watching Odo and Sephie argue about it.

Odo shrugged. "The radiation wouldn't kill them for the same reason a rattlesnake isn't killed by its own poison. That's using your brain."

"Even if that were true, which it's not, beams of radiation don't make buildings explode or melt tanks and airplanes. It would just make them radioactive, possibly knocking out their electronics with an electromagnetic pulse."

Odo said, "I know what an EMP is. I also noticed you weren't reading your book during the movie."

"The movie was so dreadful I couldn't stop watching it. After a while I stopped counting the mistakes in it."

Odo laughed. "That's why it was so good. The crazy science was hilarious. Let's go to my house. It's sunny out, we can hang out on the front steps."

Silas said, "I've been thinking about something. What does anyone think about a secret handshake?"

Emmy gave him a puzzled look. "What do you mean?"

"For the Odd Squad. We could have a secret handshake, something cool, a complicated one that would be hard to learn, but nothing too obvious."

Odo looked dubious. "Secret handshakes are used to identify members of a secret society, members you don't know. We don't need to identify ourselves to each other."

"I know, but the Odd Squad is definitely a secret society, so we should have one."

"But there are only four members, and we all know each other. We all know all the members, so there's no need for a secret handshake. I can just look at you and say, 'Oh, look, it's Silas, he's one of the four members of the Odd Squad'. You don't have to give me a secret handshake to identify yourself as a member."

"All very true and a highly logical argument, but it just seems like we should have one. Maybe if we get more members. It would be really cool to have our own secret handshake."

"I guess so." Odo glanced up at the bright sun, taking off his jacket. He stretched his arms out. "Whew, kind of warm out. Definitely don't need to be wearing a jacket."

Sephie gave him a curious look. "Why is your tee shirt so small?"

"What? It's not small, it just looks small because I've

been lifting weights, gaining a lot of muscle mass, getting abs."

Sephie, Silas, and Emmy all burst out laughing.

"What's so funny? I've been lifting weights."

"When did you start?"

Odo hesitated. "A while ago."

Silas snorted. "Yesterday?"

Sephie grabbed the back of Odo's shirt, reading the label. "It's a size small, Odo Whitley. You're wearing a kid's tee shirt."

"Fine, it's a small. But I am lifting weights, getting in shape."

Sephie grinned. "I think that's great. We'll sit here on the steps while you go in and get us some snacks. I'm hungry again."

Silas said, "Let me know if you need any help carrying the snacks. Cookies can be pretty heavy, you don't want to strain yourself."

"Very funny."

Odo ran inside, the three friends taking a seat on the front steps.

Sephie said, "Odo is so funny. I think it's great he's getting in shape though. I should do something like that."

Silas whispered, "Speaking of getting into shape, check out that old guy with the cane. I think the tortoise is definitely going to win the race."

Sephie turned to see an old white haired man in a wrinkled brown suit hobbling slowly down the sidewalk toward them. He was mumbling to himself, stopping every few feet to look up at the sky.

Emmy said, "That's kind of sad. He's so old and he's talking to himself. We shouldn't make fun of him, Silas. That could be you in fifty years."

"More like a hundred and fifty."

Emmy glared at him. "It's not funny."

The old man had almost reached the front steps when Odo stepped out with a tray of cookies, spotting the white haired man. He stopped, calling out, "Hey, Harold, how's it going? Where are you walking to today?"

The old man stopped, looking around. "Who said that?"

"Up here, it's me, Odo Whitley. You walk past here a lot and we always say hello."

The old man looked in Odo's direction, trying to focus. "Did we used to work together? How come you're so hard to see?"

"I'm translucent, remember? We never worked together, I'm still in school. Where are you walking to today?"

Harold looked confused for a moment, then said, "I'm walking to the moon." He pointed up to a pale full moon in the bright blue sky. "Nice sunny day for it. No sun on the dark side of the moon though. I don't want any part of that. No sir, the dark side of the moon is not for me." He chuckled to himself.

"Nice, sounds like fun, strolling around on the moon.

Bring me back a moon rock if you find one. They're worth a zillion dollars."

The smile faded from Harold's face. "There's a dinosaur in my house. It's eating all my food. It's a dreadful annoyance."

"Did you say a dinosaur is eating your food?"

"What did you say you wanted me to bring you?"

"A moon rock."

"That's it." Harold pulled a small notebook and a pencil from his pocket. "I'll write it down so I don't forget. What was your name again?"

"Odo Whitley."

"Right, I've got it written down so I won't forget. Moon rock for Odo Whitley, 11949 Asper Street."

"Have fun on your walk."

"Don't get eaten by a daspletosaurus!" Harold laughed, rapping his cane on the sidewalk.

Odo grinned. "Good one. I'll watch out for them. See you later, Harold."

The four friends watched Harold walk slowly down the sidewalk, stopping to look up at the moon. He pulled something from his coat pocket, turning back to them. "Oatmeal raisin cookie, my favorite. It's my lucky day!"

Odo called out, "They're my favorite too!"

Sephie looked at Odo. "That was so nice of you to talk to him like that."

"It's Harold, he's really funny. I like him. His memory is getting worse though. He always says he's walking to weird places like the moon."

"What's a daspletosaurus?"

"Some kind of dinosaur?"

Silas said, "He thinks there's a dinosaur in his house? He sounds kind of loopy."

Sephie said, "It's odd that he can't remember your name for two minutes, but he can remember a name like daspletosaurus."

"Why would he say a dinosaur is eating his food?"

Emmy said, "My grandpa had dementia and used to say strange things, get really confused. He could remember things from a long time ago, but not things that just happened, and he imagined a lot of stuff. It was really sad."

"That would explain it. He probably ate the food, then forgot and thought someone else ate it."

"But why would he say a dinosaur ate it?"

Odo shrugged. "Maybe he likes dinosaurs. He could have watched a show about them and gotten confused, thought the show was real or something. Thought there was a dinosaur in his house."

Silas looked at Emmy. "I wasn't trying to be mean when I was saying how old he was. I didn't know your grandpa had dementia. That's really sad. I'm sorry."

"It was sad, and I know you weren't being mean, you were just trying to be funny."

Sephie turned to Odo. "You never told me what happened to you when you opened your bedroom door in our beach dream."

Chapter 4

Albert's New Car

Silas said, "You're saying you both had the same dream at the same time? You were in the dream together on a little tropical island?"

Sephie nodded. "It was amazing, we were sitting on a beautiful sunny beach with palm trees and white sand and birds, and I was sitting in a beach chair reading an old hand written journal about Antarctica."

"Antarctica? Whose journal was it?"

"I don't know. I can't remember anything about it except it was really exciting and full of adventure."

Odo said, "I was watching a green bird run along the beach and said I was glad I didn't have a beak because it would be hard to eat cookies, but good if you could use it like a straw."

Silas looked confused. "What?"

"Forget the green bird, Odo Whitley. Tell them the part about your bedroom door."

"Oh, a white door appeared behind me. It was my bedroom door. I could tell because it had a chip in the glass door knob, and it was scratched from when Watson the Cat tried to escape from my room. I was keeping him there so my dad wouldn't find out I had a time traveling translucent cat in my–"

"Odo Whitley, you need to focus."

"Right. I opened the door, walked into my bedroom and found a glowing medallion on my pillow. It looked valuable, with a big blue gemstone that could have been a sapphire. I was going to give it to Sephie, but when I opened the door again a giant lizard creature pulled me into this crazy creepy jungle. It chased me for a while, and I saw all these alien lizard people in high tech antigrav vehicles racing toward a giant blue portal inside a huge transparent dome. They were all trying to escape from something."

"From what?"

"Giant erupting volcanoes. There were crazy earthquakes that knocked me over and I kept getting stabbed by weird thorny trees. The sky was black and I could see lava shooting up into the clouds of ash. I got knocked over by an earthquake and when I looked up I saw about a billion molten flaming boulders screaming down from the sky, coming right at me."

"What happened?"

Odo shrugged. "I woke up in my bed."

"Scary dream."

"Except it wasn't a dream, I was in a real world. I was solid, not translucent. It was just like when I saw Charon the Ferryman in my vision about the Plane of Percupio. It was definitely a real world."

"But you didn't wake up in the Void like you did in your Percupio vision, you woke up in your bed, like a normal dream."

"I know, but this morning I found a two-inch long thorn in my pants pocket, the same kind that stabbed my arm in the dream. I have no idea how it got in my pocket."

"Whoa. You brought something back with you?"

Odo nodded. "It's in my sock drawer. The trunk of the tree looked like a giant stabby pineapple."

"Send me a picture of the thorn and I'll do some research. I can talk to my grandpa. He knows a lot about alien plants."

Emmy said, "Do you think it means we're going there? Like when you had the vision about Percupio and we went there? It sounds like a dangerous world, with all those earthquakes and volcanoes and giant lizards."

"It was dangerous. And it had big insects in it, super creepy ones."

Emmy frowned. "I don't like big insects. They're worse than weasels."

"Spiders are the worst, but I didn't see any. It was really scary though. A big creepy flying insect landed on my chest. It was so bad. I thought it was going to bite my neck."

"That sounds scary. Do you think it had anything to

do with Sephie's journal about Antarctica?"

"I don't think so. It wasn't at all like Antarctica. It was a high tech alien world with lizard people, and it was a jungle world, warm and humid. No ice or snow and no penguins."

"Sounds like a good place not to visit."

Odo nodded. "Once was enough for me. The claws on that lizard were huge."

Half an hour later Sephie said, "I should get going, I have to help my mom with some stuff."

Silas said, "I have to go too. Don't forget to send me a picture of the thorn you brought back from the jungle world."

"I won't. See you."

That evening after dinner, Odo was in the kitchen doing his homework when he heard the sound of a car pulling into their driveway. He peered outside, watching Albert climb out of a shiny new red sedan, wiping a speck of dirt off the side mirror.

"Whoa!" Odo darted out the front door, calling out, "Did you get a new car? Does Mom know about it?"

"It's a company car. All the senior managers at Chocko CrunchCakes get them." He grinned at Odo.

"You got the promotion? And a cool new car? Can I drive it to school?"

Albert's smile vanished. "It's for business use only. Even if you had a driver's license, which you don't, you still couldn't drive it. I'm the only one who can drive it, no exceptions. Not even your mom can drive it. This is a big responsibility, Odo. It's not a toy."

"Can you drive me to school and pretend to be my chauffeur? You could wear a black hat and open the door for me."

Albert frowned. "This is not a joking matter. Open the garage door, please."

Odo ran over and raised the heavy door, standing back as his dad eased the car into the garage, parking it.

Albert stepped out and pulled the garage door down, carefully locking it. "One day you'll have your own car and understand what a big responsibility it is."

"Did you get a big raise? Maybe we should get a family computer. We could keep it in my room so it doesn't clutter up the house."

"We don't need a big fancy computer. Don't mention the new car to your mom, I want to surprise her."

"You and mom should take a cool vacation."

"And leave you here so you can have wild parties with your friends?"

"Of course not, I'd go with you. I was thinking a Caribbean island would be nice, maybe stay in a super fancy five star resort hotel. I could take surfing lessons, go scuba diving, probably rent a moped. I've always wanted to go parasailing behind a boat."

Albert gave an exasperated groan. "Enough."

After dinner Odo went up to his room, retrieving the mysterious thorn from his sock drawer, sending a picture of it to Silas.

A few minutes later he got a text back.

Amazing — I'll do some research on it and talk to my grandpa

Two hours later Odo's phone rang. It was Silas.

"You said the tree trunk looked like a giant pineapple?"

"A really big one, and it was covered with big curved stabby thorns."

"I'm sending you a picture from one of my grandpa's books."

Odo's phone beeped and he scrolled down to the image, his jaw dropping. "That's it! It's the same kind of tree except the ones I saw were a lot bigger. What is it?"

"It's called a cycad, one of the oldest plants known to man. They've been around since before the dinosaurs. They still have them in places like Africa and Australia, really warm places. Mostly they grow around the equator."

"Why would they be growing on a high tech alien lizard world?"

"I don't know. Maybe an alien planet exploded and cycad seeds got blasted into space and landed on Earth."

"That sounds a little improbable, but I guess it could happen. It doesn't help us figure out where I went though."

"We should go talk to Wikerus Praevian and Mrs. Preke."

"Wikerus always says we have to figure stuff out on our own, that he can't alter the chain of events. It's so annoying that he knows what's going on but he won't tell us."

"I'll do some more research on it, see if I find anything new."

"I'm going to wear my Serendipity Salvage work ring on Saturday, see what happens, maybe I'll get some clues."

"Good idea. Keep your eyes open for those weird co-incidences."

"I'll probably meet an old explorer from Antarctica who grows cycad trees in his backyard."

"And he has a pet daspletosaurus named Harold."

Chapter 5

Oops!

Saturday morning arrived after an uneventful week for the Odd Squad. Silas hadn't been able to find any more information about cycads, but he did learn there was nothing about their DNA to suggest the plant had an alien origin.

Odo hopped out of bed when his alarm went off. This was going to be a work ring day. He threw his clothes on, pulled open the top dresser drawer and grabbed a small black box from the back right corner. He flipped the box open, studying the shiny silver work ring.

When Mrs. Preke had hired him at Serendipity Salvage, she had given him the work ring, along with five crisp new one hundred dollar bills as his monthly retainer. She told him to wear the ring when he wanted to work, and take it off when he was done working. It had taken him some time to realize that the ring caused a series of strange coincidental events to occur, events which guided him to curious and unforeseen destinations. Sometimes he would meet new people, sometimes find curious objects. The first time he wore it, the ring had led him to Sephie's house, then sent both of them to Wikerus Praevian's spooky old Victorian mansion on Expergo Street.

He read the small inscription on the inner surface of the ring.

aperi oculos tuos et vide

It was Sephie who had translated the Latin phrase for him, *open your eyes and see*.

Odo slipped the ring onto his finger and waited. It didn't take long for the curious events to begin.

Albert's voice rang out from the kitchen. "Odo!"

Odo ran downstairs, calling out, "Odo Whitley is in the–"

Albert had an annoyed look on his face. "What did I tell you about yelling every time you come into the kitchen? I can hear you coming down the stairs."

"Sorry. Did you want something?"

Albert said, "I've never told you this before, but I used to be an excellent bowler when I was younger."

"Really?"

Petunia nodded. "He was very good. He played in a league and they won lots of awards."

"Nice. So you want me to…"

"On Friday afternoon I was invited to join the Chocko CrunchCakes bowling team by another senior manager. I've been told it's quite an honor to be asked, so I accepted. It's also a good career move, getting to know the other managers, networking, that sort of thing."

"Right. So you want me to…"

Albert frowned. "I want you to go into the garage and get my old bowling ball from the loft. The ladder is a bit rickety, not safe for a full grown adult to climb."

"No problem." Odo got up and grabbed the garage door key from the hook next to the front door, heading outside.

"I wonder where the ring is sending me? Maybe I'll find an old handwritten journal about Antarctica in the loft, written by some crazy distant relative I've never heard of."

He stepped into the garage, wiggling the ladder back and forth. "A bit shaky, but it doesn't seem too bad. Not sure it would hold my dad though." He climbed up into the cluttered loft, eyeing the old packing boxes and dusty furniture. "Why do they keep all this old junk? I don't see a bowling ball. It's probably in a box or a bag or something."

He cleared a path to the back of the loft, pushing aside some of the boxes, reading the labels. "That looks promising." Odo grabbed a brown leather satchel with black plastic handles. "It's heavy enough." He unzipped it, peering inside. "Bingo."

He reached into the bag and pulled out a red speckled bowling ball. "I'd probably be good at bowling. It doesn't seem that hard, just rolling a ball down an alley at a bunch of pins, knocking them over. How hard could that be? Maybe I should go sometime. We could all go, it would be fun." He set the ball down, his eyes on a partially opened cardboard box labeled *Albert's Trophies*.

"Must be Dad's bowling trophies." Odo grabbed one, pulling it out. "It's a guy running, not bowling." He read the small brass plaque on the base of the trophy.

1st Place One Mile Run
Albert Whitley
Track Team
Bedford Falls High School

"No way, Dad used to be on the track team? And he won a race?" Odo eyed the box of trophies. "It looks like he won a bunch of races. That's crazy. I can't imagine him being a runner."

That was the moment Odo Whitley felt the loft floor vibrating, heard the low rumbling sound. He twisted around just in time to see the red bowling ball rolling toward the edge of the loft. His insides turned to ice when he remembered that directly below the loft was his dad's shiny new company car. He let out a screech, sprawling wildly across the floor trying to grab the ball before it rolled over the edge. He didn't and it did.

When the bowling ball hit the car's windshield it made an odd crunchy sound that would hold a special place in Odo's memory for the rest of his life. With great trepidation he peered over the edge, his stomach twisting into painful knots when he saw the shattered windshield, the bowling ball resting on the car's dashboard. "I'm dead. I'm so dead. Deader than dead. I'll have to run away. Move to Antarctica. I won't go to college. I'll never get a computer." Odo's mind was spinning wildly out of control. He pulled out his phone and called Sephie, telling her what happened, sending her a photo of the windshield. "Can you fix it? Can you shape a new windshield using your powers? Can you fix it?"

"I can't shape something like that. I don't know the exact size and shape of it to make it fit right."

"What am I going to do? This is way worse than when Watson the Cat knocked Dad's work camera off the table and he thought I did it. I'm so dead. I'll have to spend the rest of my life in my room. He loves this car. He's going to go crazy, he's going to–"

"Odo Whitley, you need to calm down. Go tell your dad what happened and tell him you'll pay to have it fixed. Tell him it was your fault and you're sorry, that you'll pay for everything. You can use your Serendipity Salvage money."

Odo gave a long sigh. "You're right. I have to be responsible, say it's my fault, pay for everything. He's always telling me that. Always. I'll do it. Even though it was actually his fault because he's the one who told me to get the bowling ball."

"Odo Whitley!"

"Fine, it was my fault."

"Let me know how it goes."

"Bye."

Odo got his brilliant idea just as he was hanging up. What if his dad never found out about the windshield, never knew what he'd done? He could call someone to come fix it right now, fix it before his dad ever saw it. That could work. It was a perfect solution to the problem. Win win. Odo grabbed his phone, doing a quick search for mobile windshield repair services.

As he was scrolling down the list, his phone buzzed. He didn't recognize the number.

"Hello?"

"This is Ralph's Windshield Repair Service, we're there in fifteen minutes or the job is free."

"You can be here in fifteen minutes?"

"We're there in fifteen minutes or we fix it for free. Our work is one hundred percent guaranteed."

"That's perfect! I live at 11949 Asper Street. The car is in the garage. Try not to make a lot of noise. Um… my dad is sleeping, I don't want to wake him."

"We'll be there in fifteen minutes or less. Guaranteed or we fix it for free."

Odo breathed out a sigh of relief. This was fantastic, his plan was working. The windshield would be repaired before his dad found out what had happened. He grinned. This was his best idea ever.

Five minutes later a white van pulled up in front of

the neighbor's house, Odo glancing at the sign on the side of the truck.

"That's it, Ralph's Windshield Repair Service!"

A tall man wearing a battered old cowboy hat and dark glasses climbed out, waving to Odo, striding over to the garage.

"You must be Odo. I'm Ralph. That the car?"

Odo nodded. "A bowling ball fell out of the loft and broke the windshield." He whispered, "I'm trying to get it fixed before my dad sees it."

Ralph gave him a wink. "Gotcha. I'll see what I can do." He looked at the car, studying the windshield. "This is your lucky day, I happen to have this very windshield in my van from another job. We'll have her done in twenty minutes."

Odo watched as Ralph removed the old windshield and cleaned off the dashboard.

"Looking good. Should be an easy fix." Ralph headed out to the van to get the replacement windshield.

Odo eyed the car, rubbing his hands together. He couldn't wait to tell Sephie about his amazing plan. She'd think he was brilliant, a genius. He turned when he heard Ralph stepping back into the garage behind him. "How long do you–"

Odo never finished his sentence. He never finished it because he was not looking at Ralph, he was looking at his dad, his face an astonishing shade of crimson.

"WHAT DID YOU DO TO MY CAR?"

41

Chapter 6

Carry On

Odo couldn't make the words come out of his mouth. "I… um… it was… I…"

Ralph stepped into the garage, setting the windshield down. "You must be Odo's dad. I'd like to congratulate you, shake your hand."

Albert stared at Ralph. "Who are you?"

"I'm Ralph, mobile windshield repair service. I wanted to congratulate you on the fine job you've done teaching your son to be so responsible. I'm very impressed. You must be a remarkable dad."

"Well, I do try to… wait, what happened here?"

"A bowling ball accidentally fell from the loft. Your son called me immediately, asking me to repair the damage. He said it was his fault and he would pay for everything. It's a rare treat to meet a young man as responsible as your son. I wish more young people had parents like you, teaching their kids such important life lessons."

The crimson color had faded from Albert's face. "Well, I have tried to teach him to be responsible, but it hasn't been easy."

"Everyone knows that raising teenagers is a difficult and often thankless task. He probably won't appreciate everything you've done until he's an adult. That's when he'll be thanking you."

"Right. Well, carry on then." Albert turned, studying Odo. "Maybe there's hope for you yet."

When Albert was gone, Ralph winked at Odo. "How'd I do?"

Odo grinned. "Amazing. He wasn't even mad."

Ralph grabbed a tube of glue from his toolbox. "Funny thing, my uncle lives about two blocks from here, Professor Harold B. Livingstone, used to be a professor of paleontology at Yale University. He's kind of famous, written a bunch of books about dinosaurs."

Odo's eyes widened. "Are you talking about Harold, the old white haired guy who walks with a cane?"

"That's him. Did he tell you not to get eaten by a daspletosaurus?"

"He always says that. He was a professor at Yale?"

"Pretty famous guy, brilliant, until the dementia set in. Kind of sad. He gets confused, forgets things."

Odo nodded. "I talk to him when I see him. He seems really nice. He said something about a dinosaur eating his food?"

"Like I said, he gets confused. We check on him when we can, but we still worry about him."

"He lives near here?"

"About two blocks down the street. I'll tell you what, I won't charge you for the windshield if you check on him once in a while, maybe twice a week, just to see how's he's doing."

"You don't have to pay me. I'd be glad to do it. I like Harold." Odo knew with one hundred percent certainty that his work ring was sending him to visit Harold. What he didn't know was why.

It wasn't until an hour later that a puzzling thought entered Odo's head. Ralph hadn't said a word about him being translucent. He could see him. That was definitely weird.

He sat down at his desk, drumming his fingers on the arm of his chair. Something else was nagging him. Ralph had called him before he had even finished scrolling down the list of windshield repair services. How was that possible? It could be some new kind of search engine algorithm so businesses could call you when you begin a search. That seemed kind of weird though. How would they know his number? It was also strange that Harold knew exactly the right things to say to Albert so he wouldn't get mad. Odo shook his head. He was probably overthinking it, it had to be the work ring that was causing all the weird coincidences. He grabbed his phone and called Sephie, telling her what had happened.

"That's amazing, Odo Whitley. You were lucky the repair guy told your dad how responsible you were. That was really nice of him."

"It's weird though. I was just starting a search for a windshield repair place when Ralph called and said he could be there in fifteen minutes. How is that possible?"

"You were wearing your work ring?"

"I was."

"That's your answer, the ring was guiding you, sending you to Harold's house. He probably would have called even if you weren't searching for a windshield repair service. I can go with you if you want."

"That would be great. I'd feel kind of funny going there alone. He might think I was a burglar or something."

"Odo Whitley, you'll never guess what happened to me. You're not going to believe it."

"What happened?"

"A boy asked me to the school dance. He said it was cool that I was so smart and we could just hang out, that it would be fun."

Odo felt like someone had turned off all the lights in his head, like he was inside a dark metal echoing drum. He couldn't think of any words. His stomach hurt.

"He said he'd seen me at school and asked someone who I was. Isn't that amazing?"

Odo's voice was a hoarse whisper. "Someone asked you to the dance?"

"I'm not going with him, Odo Whitley, I told him I had a boyfriend. It was just nice that someone would ask me out, that someone noticed me and asked who I was.

That's never happened before. Some of the kids used to call me Creepy Crumb."

Odo's thoughts were a seething maelstrom. This was terrifying. Sephie was his best friend in the world. Suppose the boy asked her again and she changed her mind. Suppose she liked him, suppose she *really* liked him? What if he was handsome and a good athlete and super smart and he told her she was beautiful and–

"Odo Whitley? Are you there?"

Fortunately for Odo, Sephie couldn't see his exploding brainwaves over the phone. "Still here. It's kind of a weird coincidence, because I was going to ask you to the dance. I just forgot to because of the bowling ball thing."

"You were going to ask me to the dance?"

"I was, I mean, I am. It would be fun. We could just hang out there. At the dance. Together."

"I'm not going with anyone else, Odo Whitley. You don't need to worry about that. It was just nice that someone asked me, that's all. You don't have to ask me to the dance."

"I know that, I thought it would be fun though. It would be like… you know… sort of a date. Maybe Silas and Emmy could go with us."

There was a silence, then Sephie said, "You're asking me out on a date?"

"I am. Because… you know…"

"What do I know, Odo Whitley?"

Odo was flailing wildly, completely out of control.

"Um… how much I like you? Stuff like that."

Sephie said, "And because of what's engraved on the gold locket that you gave me in Percupio?"

Odo groaned to himself. "Right, that too."

"I'm going to call Emmy and see if they'll go with us. Bye, Odo."

Odo slumped forward in his chair, his hands pressed against his forehead. He was going to a dance. What was he thinking? He didn't have the slightest idea how to dance. Zero. Zip. This was bad. He sat up straight, an odd thought popping into his head, something Sephie had just said. She had called him Odo, not Odo Whitley. She always called him Odo Whitley. Always. He wasn't sure what it meant or why she did it, but he liked it. He groaned again. Silas was going to murder him with a big rusty axe when Emmy told him they were all going to the school dance.

Chapter 7

The Dance

Silas had a dour expression on his face, his eyes fixed on Odo. "How come you're solid, not translucent?"

"Sephie wanted me to wear my Sinarian ring so people could see who she was dancing with." When Odo and Sephie had returned from their first adventure, a Sinarian had given each of them a ring. Odo's ring made him solid, and Sephie's ring made her translucent.

Silas was still staring at him. "What were you thinking? Why did you ask Sephie to the dance? Do you even know how to dance? Are you completely insane?"

Odo whispered, "Someone asked Sephie to the dance and I panicked. I was afraid she'd go with him if I didn't ask her, afraid she might like him because he liked going to dances. I could tell she really wanted to go."

"Oh. I thought maybe you went loopy or something. Emmy was so excited about the dance that I couldn't say no. This is bad." Silas studied the crowd of dancers on the gym floor. "Maybe we can just stand around and watch."

Sephie ran up to Odo, grabbing his arm. "Time to dance, Odo."

"I can't hear you, the music is too loud."

"Nice try. You're going to dance with me, that's why we're here. Time is money, let's go."

"I don't exactly know how to dance. At all."

Silas gazed at the dancers. "It doesn't look that hard. Just pretend you're being attacked by a swarm of Plindorian killer bees."

Odo laughed. "It does kind of look like that. Those guys over there look like they're running but they're not going anywhere."

Emmy grabbed Silas' hand, dragging him onto the dance floor.

"Let's go, Odo. If Silas can do it, you can do it. Dancing is way less scary than the murderous Stirpians we faced on Atroxia."

"Good point, no one will kill me for being a bad dancer." Odo followed Sephie onto the dance floor, doing his best impression of someone being attacked by killer Plindorian bees. It was actually kind of fun, and Sephie was laughing, not much better at dancing than Odo. He liked seeing her laugh.

Three dances later the four friends got drinks and snacks and took a seat on the bleachers.

Silas said, "Emmy's super good at dancing. She was teaching me."

Emmy shrugged. "I learned to dance in the alternate

timeline when I was one of the cool popular kids. It's not that hard and it's a lot of fun. I can teach you guys if you want."

Silas was staring into the crowd, a frown forming on his face.

Emmy said, "What's the matter? What are you looking at?"

"There's a ghost out there, and he's looking right at us."

"What kind of ghost?"

"He's wearing a big fur parka and fur boots."

"Is he dancing?"

"What? No, of course he's not dancing. Why would a ghost in a fur parka be dancing? He's just staring at us. And now he's gone. He vanished."

Odo gave a yelp. "Fur parka! Antarctica! The journal Sephie was reading in our dream."

Sephie said, "I wish I could remember what the journal was about. It was so interesting but when I woke up I'd forgotten what was in it."

"In the dream you said it was full of mystery and adventure and intrigue."

Emmy grabbed Silas' hand. "Let's go, we're here to dance, not solve spooky Antarctic ghost mysteries."

Silas turned to Odo. "See what you did? You created a dance monster."

Sephie laughed. "Two dance monsters." She grabbed Odo's hand. "Let's go, Odo. Time to show off your moves."

A curious thing happened when Odo and Sephie were dancing. A girl stepped out of the crowd, whispering something in Sephie's ear. Sephie nodded, said something, then the girl said something, shrugged, and walked away.

Odo moved closer to Sephie. "What was that about?"

"Nothing."

"What did she want? Who was that?"

"Just some girl. She was asking me what time it was."

"You didn't look at your watch and you were talking about something."

"It was nothing, so quit asking. We're here to dance, not solve mysteries."

Fifteen minutes later Silas and Emmy appeared. "We should probably get going. I don't want to miss the bus."

The four friends made their way outside, boarding the city bus, laughing for most of the ride home. Silas was doing a hilarious impression of Odo's dance moves when he stopped, his eyes on the front of the bus.

"It's the ghost in the fur parka. He has a big fur hood and a beard. I can't see his face, it's hidden in shadows."

"What does he want?"

"I don't know. I sent him a thought but he's not answering. He's watching us though."

Odo said. "We need to visit Harold and find out what this is about. I'm certain my vision of the alien jungle world is connected to Antarctica and to Harold, but I don't know how."

Odo was the last one off the bus, walking two blocks to his house in the dark. He was glad they had gone to the dance. It was way more fun than he thought it would be. You didn't have to be a good dancer to have fun and nobody cared how you danced. He ran up the front steps, stopping when he saw the small box illuminated by the porch light. The box was wrapped in brown paper, carefully tied up with green twine.

He picked it up, studying the shaky handwriting on the white tag.

Odo Whitley
11949 Asper Street
Earth

"Earth? What does that mean?" He started to open it, then stopped. Maybe it was a dangerous alien object, a waystone that would shift him to a potentially deadly world if he touched it. One of Wikerus Praevian's cardinal rules was never touch a waystone if you don't know where it's from. He jammed the box into his coat pocket and headed inside.

His mom popped out of the kitchen, a big smile on her face. "How was the dance?"

"It was a lot of fun. Way more fun than I thought it would be. Emmy's the only one who can dance, but nobody cared if you were good or not."

"Your father and I used to go dancing when we were young."

"Dad went dancing? Really?"

"Your dad has a surprise for you."

"A pair of dancing shoes?"

"Something better. He's in the kitchen."

Odo's jaw dropped when he saw the big box on the kitchen table, his dad reading an instruction booklet.

"You got a computer? No way! Really?" He darted over to the box. "Whoa, this is a super nice one. I thought you weren't going to get one?"

"Your friend Ralph got me thinking. You're going to need one for school, especially if you're going to college. Your mom's going to need one too, for the classes she'll be taking at Gardner College."

Odo raised his eyebrows.

"Your dad thinks I should keep taking classes and get a degree."

"That's amazing. Do you need any help with the computer? Silas has one just like this."

Albert handed the instruction booklet to Odo. "I use one at work but I don't have the slightest idea how to set them up."

Odo realized it was the first time his dad had ever admitted he didn't know something.

"It's a lot easier than it looks." Half an hour later the computer was set up, Odo's parents sitting in front of it.

"Look at this, I can use the computer to sign up for

my classes."

Odo grinned, running up to his room. It was time to find out what was in the mysterious brown box.

Chapter 8

The Box

Odo was sitting on his bed getting ready to open the little box when his phone rang. He grabbed it from his desk, checking the number. It was Sephie.

"Hey, what's up? I'm just about to open a weird box I found on the front steps. It's addressed to–"

"I have to tell you something, Odo, but I'm afraid to."

The box fell from Odo's hands. "You're going out with that guy. Is that it? You're breaking up with me? You like him?"

"What guy?"

"The one who asked you to the dance. You like him?"

"Why would you even think that? Of course I'm not going out with him. I already told you that."

"Oh, what is it then?"

"At the dance, remember the girl who whispered something to me?"

"She wanted to know what time it was."

"That's not what she wanted to know."

Odo's expression darkened. "Did she say something

55

mean to you?"

"She wanted to know if you were my boyfriend. She said you were super cute and she wanted to dance with you."

"She wanted to dance with me? Really?"

"She was way cuter than me. She's one of the popular girls."

"Does she have flaming orange hair?"

"No."

"Then she's not cuter than you."

"Are you just saying that?"

"Do you remember the first time we shifted to Pacalia?"

"Of course I remember. That was our first adventure."

"You told me you didn't like it when people looked at you because you were afraid of what they might be thinking about you, about how you looked. Do you remember what I said?"

"Of course I do, I was so shocked I could hardly breathe. I couldn't look at you. You just blurted it right out. You said you thought I was beautiful."

"I still think that. You're also the most amazing person I've ever met. Ever."

"I was worried because she was so cute. And popular. And she thought you were super cute."

"Not as worried as I was when that guy asked you to the dance."

"You totally surprised me. I never thought you'd be

jealous."

"Can I ask you a weird question?"

"All your questions are weird."

"Ha ha. Seriously though, you always used to call me Odo Whitley, but now you just call me Odo. How come?"

Sephie hesitated. "I don't know, it just… after you asked me to the dance it felt safe to call you Odo. I know it's kind of odd, but I was never sure if you really thought I–"

"It's not odd. I can talk to you about anything at all and not worry about it. It's amazing."

"My mom just got home, I have to go. Bye, Odo. Thanks for saying all those nice things. Really."

"Bye, Seph."

Odo set the phone down on his bed. He was glad he'd asked Sephie to the dance. It was the scariest thing and the best thing he'd ever done.

He grabbed a pair of scissors from his desk drawer and snipped the string on the mystery box, carefully removing the brown wrapping paper, lifting the lid.

"It's a rock. Who would send me a rock?" He gave it a quick tap with his finger, getting a slight tingling sensation. It was a waystone from another world, but a weak one. He picked it up, examining it. It looked volcanic, lots of little holes in it, like a sponge. It also looked strangely familiar. He grabbed his phone and did a quick search, scrolling down through a series of images.

"No way. I think it's a moon rock! I think Harold gave me a moon rock."

He took a photo of the rock and sent it to Silas. It had to be from Harold, but that was crazy. How did he get it? There's no way he walked to the moon. Maybe he was connected to the early lunar landings and one of the astronauts gave it to him. If it really was a moon rock, he had to return it, it was way too valuable, worth a fortune. Harold had probably forgotten how much moon rocks are worth.

His phone beeped. It was a text from Silas.

Is that a moon rock?????

I'm not sure. I found it on my porch addressed to me. Part of the address was 'Earth'.

Is it from Harold? It sounds like something he would say. Kind of loopy.

I'm going to take it to the museum and have someone look at it, see if it's real.

I'll go with you.

OK, see you tomorrow.

The next day after school, Odo, Sephie, and Silas took the bus to the Bedford Falls Natural History Museum, making their way through the building to the Rocks and Minerals section. Odo was solid, wearing his Sinarian ring.

They looked around, Silas spotting a heavy wooden

door marked *Curator*.

Odo rapped on the door. A few moments later it swung open, a tall man in a gray pinstripe suit and gold rimmed glasses looking down at them, clearly annoyed by their presence.

"Yes? Did you need something?"

"I have a rock I wanted someone to look at?"

"You found a rock and you want someone to look at it. Will wonders never cease."

"Right. The thing is, I think it's a moon rock."

The man gave Odo a weary look. "It's not a moon rock. Anything else? I'm very busy."

"You didn't look at it."

"I don't need to. It's not a moon rock."

Odo pulled the lid off the box. "Just look at it."

"It's simply not possible that–" The curator stopped short, his eyes fixed on the spongy looking rock. He took the box from Odo, studying the rock. "Where did you get this?"

"I found it on my porch."

The curator gave Odo a dark accusatory look. "On your porch? It's a federal crime to steal a moon rock, a very serious federal crime."

"I didn't steal it, I found it on my porch and thought it looked like a moon rock."

The curator eyed the stone. "Wait here, I'll be back in a few minutes. I need to examine this under a microscope." He took the box, closing the heavy wooden door behind him, the lock clicking shut.

Sephie had been studying the curator's brain waves. She whispered, "I don't like this. I don't trust him."

Ten minutes later the curator hadn't returned.

"What do we do if he doesn't come back?"

"We tell someone, find out where he is."

"What do we tell them, that we gave him a moon rock worth a jillion dollars and he stole it? Who's going to believe us?"

Sephie said, "I'm going to use the Traveling Eye and find out what he's doing."

"Good idea."

Sephie took a seat on a bench, closing her eyes. The Traveling Eye was a skill she had learned from their Fortisian friend Cyra on Plindor. She could move her consciousness out of her body and travel anywhere she wanted. She was able to see and hear, but couldn't interact with anyone, much like a ghost. Because consciousness is pure energy and has no physical mass, she could easily pass through walls and doors.

She floated through the heavy door into the curator's office. He was seated at his desk, whispering to someone on the phone.

"You got the pictures I sent? The rock is genuine, absolutely real, I'm certain of it. I've examined it carefully. I have no idea where the kid got it, but it's ours now. It's worth a fortune, at least six or seven million on the black market, maybe more. No, he can't do anything, he didn't

even know what it was. I'll tell him it wasn't worth anything, replace it with a common volcanic rock. They're
dumb kids, they'll believe anything I tell them."

Chapter 9

Harold's House

Sephie floated back to her physical body, her eyes blinking open. "He's going to steal it. He was talking to someone on the phone and said it's a real moon rock, worth six or seven million dollars on the black market. He called us dumb kids."

Silas frowned. "What do we do? Should we tell someone?"

Odo said, "I say we teach him a lesson and get the rock back, make sure he never calls us dumb kids again."

"How? Do you have a plan?"

"We're the Odd Squad, we always have a plan. Sephie can implant a false memory in his mind to make him leave the museum, then the incredible Translucent Boy will walk through the door and take back the moon rock."

Silas grinned. "Nice. Go Odd Squad!"

Sephie closed her eyes, opening them twenty seconds later. "It's done. He just remembered that he left a box of valuable gems on the front seat of his car and forgot to lock the car door."

Moments later the door swung open, the curator dashing out, racing down the hallway, the door clicking shut behind him.

Odo twisted the handle. "It's locked, not a problem for the incredible Translucent Boy." He took off his Sinarian ring, once again translucent, and pressed his hand against the door, a six-foot tall shimmering rectangle appearing. "I'll be back in a flash with the rock."

Odo stepped through the rippling translucent doorway into the curator's office, spotting the small brown box on his desk. "Got it." He plucked the moon rock from the box, then stopped, a grin crossing his face. Grabbing a round stone from the base of a tall potted plant, he wrapped it in tissue paper and placed it in the brown box. "That should do it."

Sephie gave a cheer when Odo stepped back through the door with the moon rock in his hand. "That will teach him not to mess with the Odd Squad."

They took the bus home, Odo and Silas imagining the look on the curator's face when he discovered the worthless river rock in the box.

"He'll probably say super rude stuff and his eyes will bug out like this."

"And he'll start pounding the desk with his fist."

Sephie laughed, then said, "Now that we have it back, it's time to visit Harold and ask him where he got the moon rock."

"Agreed."

The next day after school the four friends took the bus to Odo's house, then headed south on Asper Street.

"What's Harold's address?"

"9207 Asper Street."

"There it is, it's that big dark green house. He seriously needs to cut his lawn. I think I saw a giraffe running through the grass."

Silas snorted. "Good one."

Sephie said, "He's old and he has dementia. You can't expect him to do yard work."

"You're right, I didn't think about that. I'll come by this weekend and cut his lawn. Silas can help me."

"What?"

"What are we going to say to him? He won't remember us."

"I'll think of something. I know, we can tell him his nephew Ralph sent us. That will work."

They stepped up onto the porch, Odo ringing the bell.

Moments later the door swung open, Harold peering out, looking up and down the street. "Did anyone follow you?"

"Hi, Harold, I'm Odo–"

"You're Odo Whitley. Come in, we don't have much time."

Odo took a step back. "Harold?"

"Hurry, please, time is of the essence."

The four friends stepped into the house, Odo scanning

the musty, massively cluttered sitting room, stacks of dusty books piled on tables and chairs, the volumes spilling onto the floor, a long row of murky glass display cases filled with all manner of bones and fossils and odd prehistoric curiosities.

"Is that a dinosaur skull?"

"You're translucent. You're a shifter?"

Odo gaped at Harold. "How did you–"

Harold turned to Sephie. "Orange hair. You're a Fortisian?"

"I'm half Fortisian and half human. My dad was Fortisian."

"There's a story there, but we don't have time for it now. I don't know how much longer I'll be lucid."

Odo held out the moon rock. "Did you give me this? It was in a box addressed to me on my front porch."

Harold looked at it. "Maybe. Probably. I have a box of them. I need to give you this while I can. You need to guard it with your life."

Harold pulled a gleaming circular medallion from his pocket, handing it to Odo. In the center of the medallion was a glowing, multi-faceted blue stone resembling a sapphire.

"That's the medallion I saw in my dream! It's the same one, with rings of copper, silver, and gold around a blue gemstone."

"It's extremely old, and it's the only way you'll be able to take–"

Harold was cut short by a cacophonous crashing sound from the next room. The light seemed to fade from his eyes. "It's the only way you can take… something. Did I drop a plate?" He turned, sinking slowly down onto a dark blue couch.

"Harold?"

Harold gave a pleasant smile. "Are you Odo?"

"Yes, I'm your friend, Odo Whitley."

"Are you here about the dinosaur? He's been making a dreadful mess, eating my food."

"A dinosaur? You're sure?"

"Oh, yes, quite certain. I've seen him."

Odo took a deep breath, looking at the others. "I guess we should go in there and see what made that crashing noise."

Silas gulped. "Suppose it really is a dinosaur? It could be a velociraptor. That would be really bad. They're small, but super ferocious predators."

Odo crept forward, the others behind him. "It came from in there." He inched the door open, peeking into the kitchen, checking for movement. "Whatever it was is gone."

They entered the kitchen, Emmy grimacing, pointing to the floor. "Something was eating that fish. Look how big the bite marks are."

Silas studied it. "I think it's a salmon. What could do that? There are big chunks bitten out of it."

"The refrigerator door is open. It must have pulled the

fish out and knocked over those plates."

"I don't like this. Why would he say it was a dinosaur?"

Silas' eyes were wide. He was staring at something behind Odo. "You're not going to like this."

Odo whipped around. "What is it?"

"It's the ghost in the fur parka. He's standing in the doorway, motioning for us to follow him."

Emmy whispered, "Could this possibly get any stranger?"

"I think it's about to. Follow me."

They stepped back into the living room, Silas leading the way. Harold was sitting on the couch reading a book. He glanced up at them. "You're Odo! Are these your friends?"

"They are. This is Sephie, Silas, and Emmy. We're looking for the dinosaur."

"Excellent. Such a nuisance, eating all my food."

Silas whispered, "The ghost is pointing to the stack of books on top of that glass case." He grabbed a chair, moving it next to the display case, hopping up onto it. "Is it something up here? You want us to find something up here?"

Silas raised a tattered red book. "This? No?" He held up another one. "This one?"

Sephie let out a yelp when he picked up the third book. "That's the journal I was reading in my dream!"

Chapter 10

The Journal

Silas jumped down from the chair, glancing around the room. "The ghost is gone." He handed the dusty leather bound book to Sephie.

Sephie flipped open the front cover, studying the first page. "It's written by Dr. Stanley B. Livingstone. It's a journal about an expedition to Antarctica in 1944, during the Second World War."

Harold called out, "That's my father's journal. Stanley Livingstone was my father. He used to give me presents when I was a child, but I don't know where he is. He didn't come home."

Sephie stepped over to Harold. "Harold, would you mind if we borrowed your father's journal for a few days? We'd love to know more about him. He must have been a remarkable person. We'll bring it right back when we're done reading it."

"Oh, yes, he was a great adventurer. You're quite welcome to read it. I don't know where he is. No one does."

"I understand. Your nephew told Odo that they come

and check on you a few times a week?"

"I don't have a nephew."

"You don't have a nephew named Ralph?"

Harold shook his head. "Or any other name. I'm an only child, I don't have any nieces or nephews. I'm hungry. I'm going to make some dinner. I go to bed early. Early to bed and early to rise."

Sephie said, "How about I make you a sandwich and we'll clean up the kitchen? Some dishes fell on the floor. It's kind of a mess in there."

"It's that dinosaur. He's eating my food. Such a dreadful nuisance. I like tuna fish."

"You sit here and I'll make you a nice tuna sandwich."

Half an hour later the kitchen was tidied up and Harold had finished his lunch. "Excellent sandwich. I like tuna fish. I think I always have."

Odo pulled the medallion from his pocket, showing it to Harold. "Do you remember this? You told me to take care of it."

"My father gave me that on my tenth birthday. He used to bring me such nice presents."

"Do you know what it does?"

"I don't think it does anything. It's a medallion."

"You were a professor of paleontology at Yale?"

"You're right, I think I was. Isn't that marvelous? I have lots of books and a big collection of fossils. Now that I think about it, I was a full professor of paleontology at Yale for many years. Such a lovely time it was. I wrote more than a few books. It seems so long ago, but also like it was yesterday. Oh, there's a letter in the back of the journal. I don't think you're supposed to open it until I tell you."

"A letter?"

"Time for bed. I go to bed early and get up early, and I always have a healthy breakfast. It's very important to have a nutritious breakfast. I always have an egg and a muffin. I put strawberry jam on the muffin, but not too much jam. Too much sugar is bad for you. I put a pinch of salt on the egg."

"Okay, we'll bring the journal back in a day or two, I promise."

Odo said, "You said you had a box of moon rocks? Do you remember where you got them?"

"From the moon. Where else would I get moon rocks? Certainly not from Mars or Venus." He gave a cheerful laugh.

Silas grabbed Odo's arm, whispering, "I know who he is!"

"Who who is?"

Silas leaned over, whispering to the others. "The ghost in the fur parka is Harold's father, Dr. Stanley B. Livingstone. I think he died in Antarctica and he wants us to read the journal."

Sephie glanced over at Harold. "We should go, Harold needs to go to bed."

The friends said their goodbyes to Harold and headed

outside.

"I can't wait to read this. I remember how interesting it was in my dream. I couldn't put it down."

Odo said, "Is there a letter in the back?"

She flipped the journal open, pulling out a sealed brown envelope, holding it up for the others to see.

For Odo Whitley and his friends
DO NOT OPEN

"This is so confusing. When did he write the letter?"

"Probably today. He was completely lucid when we got there. He knew you were a shifter and I was a Fortisian."

"How could he possibly know about that stuff? He studies dinosaurs."

"I don't know, but we're going to find out."

"He said the medallion was the only way to do something, but he didn't say what."

"Maybe the letter will explain it."

"I hope so. Text me if you find something good in the journal."

"Okay."

Harold had told him to guard the medallion with his life, so the first thing Odo did when he got home was to hide the medallion in a safe place. He placed his hand on the wall of his bedroom, a small section of it becoming translucent. Reaching through the wall, he set the medallion on a heavy wooden crossbeam. He removed his hand, the wall solid again. "It should be safe in there."

The next thing he did was to run downstairs and get on the new computer, searching for Ralph's Mobile Windshield Repair Service.

"Harold might be mistaken about not having a nephew. He might have forgotten, or maybe Ralph isn't an actual blood relative. Maybe Ralph calls him Uncle Harold, but he's not a real uncle. Or maybe Harold was married, and Ralph was his wife's nephew. That could be it."

After fifteen minutes of searching, Odo gave up. "Nothing. Zip. Not a single Ralph's Windshield Repair Service within a hundred miles of Bedford Falls. I knew there was something seriously off about him. He called too soon, came over too fast, and manipulated my dad into not being mad at me. The question is, who is he and why did he want me to meet Harold? I wish I knew what was eating the salmon in Harold's kitchen. Those were huge bites, like a giant Alaskan grizzly bear was eating it. Why would Harold say it was a dinosaur? Maybe it was someone's pet lizard that escaped and got into his house."

Odo sighed. If it was a pet lizard, it would have been there when they entered the kitchen. And how could a lizard open the refrigerator door? Whatever the thing was, it was smart enough to hide from them and big enough to open the refrigerator and take out the salmon.

The last thing he did was do a search for Dr. Stanley B. Livingstone. It didn't take long to find him.

"Here it is. It says Stanley B. Livingstone was a distinguished geologist who worked with the military during World War II on a number of classified projects in Antarctica. He was the sole survivor of an expedition that ended in tragedy, caught unawares by a sudden ferocious gale force blizzard. After the war ended he went back to Antarctica by himself and was never heard from again."

Odo shut off the computer, heading up to his room. "I wonder why he went back there? And why did he go back alone? That seems kind of crazy. Maybe Sephie will learn something from the journal."

Odo went upstairs and crawled into bed, drifting off into a deep sleep, blissfully unaware of the text that arrived in the middle of the night.

Odo! You're not going to believe what I found in the journal! It's incredible! I know where Harold's father got the medallion! He found it in Antarctica during World War II. I don't want to say anything else in case someone reads this. I'll tell you at lunch. We have to go see Harold. We have to talk to him about his father and about the letter in the journal.

Chapter 11

Incredible!

The four friends met in the school cafeteria the next day, Silas setting his tray down across from Odo. "Pizza day. Yum."

"Sephie found something in Harold's Antarctica journal. She sent me a text in the middle of the night saying it's incredible, that she knows where Harold's dad found the medallion."

Emmy took a seat next to Silas. "This pizza looks undercooked. And by undercooked I mean raw. And by raw I mean disgusting."

"There's no such thing as bad pizza. I'll eat yours if you don't want it."

"No one likes soggy raw pizza."

Odo frowned. "Did you hear what I said? Sephie found something incredible in the journal."

Sephie sat down next to Odo, looking at his plate. "The pizza looks soggy."

Silas said, "What did you find in the journal?"

Sephie leaned forward, her voice a low whisper.

"Harold's dad was a geologist working with the military during World War II. He went on an expedition to Antarctica to survey a section of the ice sheet that covers the continent. They were searching for a good location to build a secret underground military facility."

Silas said, "The ice sheet can be over a mile thick. How could they build an underground facility?"

"Stanley didn't know the purpose of the underground base or how they were going to build it, but he suspected it was a secret submarine base."

"You're right, that is incredible."

"That's not the incredible part. His group was caught in a huge blizzard, with winds over a hundred and fifty miles an hour. He was driving a snow cat and got separated from the others, got lost and drove into a deep crevasse hidden under a layer of ice and snow. The snow cat tumbled a few hundred feet down and got lodged between the ice walls. That saved his life. He managed to climb out a window and he could see to the bottom of the crevasse, hundreds of feet below him. There were lights shining up from below."

"What kind of lights?"

"I'm getting to that. He had ice climbing gear with him, but instead of climbing back up into the deadly blizzard, he decided to climb down and investigate the mysterious lights. When he reached the bottom of the crevasse he was standing on top of a gigantic transparent dome made out of an unknown synthetic material, the top of the dome about five hundred feet above ground level. He used his climbing ropes to lower himself through a crack in the dome onto the top of a building."

"A building? In a dome under the Antarctic ice?"

"And that's not the incredible part." She grinned at Odo. "Do you want to hear the incredible part?"

"Of course I do. Hurry up and tell us."

"He entered the building and took a set of stairs down to the ground level, stepping out into an abandoned ancient high tech city. Some of the lights were still working after who knows how many thousands of years. He said the dome was at least three or four miles wide. He also said some of the buildings were solid, but some of them he called ghost buildings because his hand would pass right through them like they weren't there. He found the medallion when he was exploring the inside of a ghost building. It was attached to a suit of clothing made of an indestructible synthetic fabric. A big suit of clothing eight or nine feet long."

"That's the incredible part?"

"That's not the incredible part."

Odo's eyes narrowed.

"Did I mention he found skeletons?"

"What kind of skeletons?"

"Ten-foot tall skeletons with big heads, two arms and two legs."

"No way! Alien skeletons in Antarctica? That's not possible."

"He also found four dinosaur skeletons and he took pictures of everything. The photos might be tucked away somewhere in Harold's house. We could look for them."

"That was the incredible part?"

"Not quite."

Silas laughed when he saw the expression on Odo's face.

Sephie put her hand on Odo's arm. "Okay, here it is, this is the incredible part. There was a huge shimmering blue portal like the one in your vision, the one the aliens were using to escape from the volcanoes."

Odo's jaw dropped. "No way!"

Silas said, "You're saying there was an alien city in Antarctica during the time of the dinosaurs?"

"That's what it looks like."

"What happened to Stanley?"

"He climbed out of the crevasse after the storm ended and managed to make it back to their base camp, never telling anyone about the dome city. He was planning to go back after the war and investigate it. That's where his journal ends."

Odo said, "I did some research on him last night. It said he went back to Antarctica on his own after the war but he was never heard from again. He must have died there."

"That's so sad. That's why Harold keeps saying nobody knows where Stanley is. He lost his dad when he was young."

77

"Do you think that's why Harold became a paleontologist?"

"It would make sense if he read his dad's journal. Stanley described three or four of the dinosaur skeletons and drew sketches of them. One of them looked like a small T-rex."

"Harold probably grew up wanting to learn more about what his dad saw there."

"We still don't know what the medallion is for."

Emmy said, "And there's another big problem. In Odo's vision the blue portal was surrounded by a hot humid jungle, not snow and ice and blizzards. He wasn't in Antarctica."

Silas said, "Two words, continental drift."

"What's that?"

"Back when there were dinosaurs there weren't seven continents like there are now, there was one big supercontinent called Pangaea, stretching all the way from the North Pole to the South Pole. The rest of the world was all ocean. Over a few hundred million years Pangaea split apart into the continents we know today. Thanks to mega volcanoes and giant monster earthquakes, the pieces of Pangaea slowly drifted away from each other across the Earth's mantle. If you look at a world map, the continents look like puzzle pieces that fit together."

"What does all that mean?"

"It means the aliens built the dome city in the jungles of Pangaea, and a hundred and fifty million years later,

Stanley discovered the lost city under the frozen Antarctic ice sheet."

Sephie nodded. "Silas is right. I was researching it last night. It said supercontinents like Pangaea form every five hundred million years."

"There were other supercontinents besides Pangaea?"

Sephie nodded. "Rodinia was about a billion years ago, and Pannotia was six hundred million years ago."

"That's crazy."

"I also read that there wasn't any ice on Antarctica until about thirty-four million years ago."

Odo looked dubious. "There's no way a city could last that long. No way."

"A city built by humans couldn't, but Stanley said there was something strange about the city, some of the buildings were there, but not there. The city wasn't built out of stone and glass and metal, it was built from something else, something we don't understand."

Odo said, "I'm getting a headache. I need to eat something, like this delicious soggy pizza."

Silas looked at Emmy's plate. "Are you going to eat that disgusting undercooked pizza?"

"You're not getting my pizza." She turned to Odo. "So the place you visited wasn't an alien world, it was Earth. You visited Pangaea a hundred and fifty million years ago and you saw dinosaurs."

Odo grinned at Sephie. "And *that* is the incredible part."

Chapter 12

Odo's Discovery

Odo woke up the next morning, his thoughts on the puzzle of Pangaea and the myriad of unanswered questions. Why was the Odd Squad being pulled into this strange adventure? What were they supposed to do? What was Harold's part in all this? Why had Ralph the windshield repair guy wanted him to meet Harold? Who *was* Ralph? What was the blue medallion for? Harold said it was the only way to do something, but he hadn't said what. And who or what had been eating the salmon in Harold's kitchen? Odo stopped short, slapping his hand to his forehead.

"Ralph's phone number is on my phone!" He ran to his desk and grabbed his phone, scrolling down through the recent calls. "There it is, that's the number he called from. Let's see what Ralph the friendly mobile windshield repair guy has to say when I tell him Harold doesn't have a nephew."

Odo dialed the number, frowning when he heard a series of clicking sounds, the line abruptly going dead.

Odo groaned. "Why is everything always so complicated?" He slumped down onto his bed. "I should look at the medallion again. There has to be something I'm missing."

He stood up, pressing his hand against the wall, reaching through and grabbing the medallion. Taking a seat at his desk, he examined the medallion with his big magnifying glass.

"Each ring around the stone is made of a different metal, copper, silver, and gold. Nothing too weird about that. The blue jewel in the center could be a sapphire, but it glows in the dark. Glow in the dark objects usually have phosphors in them, particles that absorb sunlight, then radiate it back out again over time. Since the medallion is still glowing after being in the dark for two days, it can't be phosphors. They used to paint watch dials with luminous paint containing radium-226, but this doesn't look at all like that. I can see something glowing underneath the gem, but I can't tell exactly what it is. It could be electronics, maybe microchips or LEDs. Or more likely some crazy high tech stuff I've never seen before. I should take it to school and look at it under a microscope in science class."

"Odo! Breakfast!"

"Okay!" Odo pulled his clothes on, slipping the medallion into his pocket. He ran down the stairs and into the kitchen. "Where's Dad?"

"He had to go in early today. He's very busy with the

new line of Golden CrunchCakes."

"How does he like his new job?"

"He likes being a senior manager, and he loves the new car. He's very proud of it."

Petunia set a plate of eggs and toast in front of Odo.

"It's cool that he got the promotion and the new car. You said he wants you to get a degree?"

Petunia nodded. "I was shocked. He said we're not getting any younger, and we should do what we want to do while we still can. That's why he got you the computer, and why he said we should take a nice tropical vacation. He wants you to go to college and graduate. He had to drop out of college after one year because we couldn't afford it. He never talks about it, but I know it bothers him. A lot of the people he works with have college degrees."

"Maybe he could go back to school and get a degree. The new computer is amazing. Did he say anything else about the windshield?"

Petunia shook her head. "He was proud of you for fixing it. He said you were being responsible."

Odo jumped up, grabbing a piece of toast. "Bus is here, gotta go!"

"Have a good day, King Odo."

"Bye!" Odo darted out the front door, slamming it behind him. He was glad his mom was taking classes. She seemed happier, more confident. Maybe his dad would go back to school sometime and get a degree.

He made his way to the back of the school bus, grabbing an overhead rail, his tried and true method of avoiding unwanted collisions with students who didn't notice him. He could wear his Sinarian ring and be solid like everyone else, but he'd gotten used to being translucent and had come to appreciate the extra time it gave him to read and think during school. He pressed his hand against the medallion in his pocket, his thoughts turning to Harold. Harold had told him he didn't think the medallion did anything, but when he was lucid he told Odo to guard it with his life. Why? That was the big question. Maybe his letter would explain everything.

Odo waited until the other kids had exited the bus, then hopped off, entering the school through the main doors. The bell had already rung so the hallways were empty, eliminating the possibility of inadvertent collisions with oblivious students. As he strolled down the long empty corridor, he started thinking about the dream he and Sephie had shared, wondering exactly where they had been. Was it a dream? Was it real? He couldn't remember if he'd been solid or translucent. It was a beautiful beach, with white sand that sparkled in the sun, blue skies, the blue green sea dotted with hundreds of small islands, the waves breaking on the shore like clockwork, the green bird running across the beach for–

Odo stopped short. Something was off. He looked down at the ground, his eyes widening. "I'm walking in sand. Why am I walking in sand?" He looked up, gaping at a translucent green bird racing across the floor, the hallway ceiling now a curious shade of sky blue. Moments later the sand and the bird were gone, the tiled hallway floor visible again.

The medallion in his pocket felt warm, almost hot. His jaw dropped when he pulled it out to look at it. The sapphire was flaring brightly, now an intense shade of violet. He watched as the violet light faded, the gem cooling rapidly, returning to its original sapphire blue color.

Odo headed to his class, his mind a whirlwind. What had just happened? He'd been thinking about the beach from his dream and thirty seconds later he was walking in white sand. The medallion had gotten hot, flaring with a violet light. When he stopped walking, the sand faded away, the hallway floor returning, the green bird gone. This was incredible. If he was right, it meant the medallion was some kind of high tech interstellar shifting device activated by his thoughts.

He stepped into his homeroom and took a seat, the teacher taking little notice of translucent Odo. He pulled the medallion from his pocket, studying it. This was an astonishing development, one that would explain why Harold had said he was walking to the moon. At one time Harold must have known the purpose of the medallion, but his growing dementia had caused him to forget. When he was lucid and remembered what the medallion did, he had told Odo to guard it with his life. But guard it for what? What were they supposed to do with it?

Where were they supposed to go?

He met the others at lunch, telling them what he had discovered.

Emmy was examining the medallion, turning it over in her hand, studying it. "You're saying you can visit another world just by thinking about it?"

"I think so. The beach was starting to appear, but when I stopped walking, it faded away. That's why Harold said he was walking to the moon."

Silas grinned. "We should test it after school, go to that beach. Does anyone have a surfboard?"

Emmy frowned. "It doesn't sound safe. How do we get back from the beach world?"

"Maybe we think about our world?"

"Maybe we think about it? Suppose that's not it, suppose we can't get back?"

"Harold always got back."

"He might know something about the medallion that we don't know. There might be a trick to getting back."

Sephie said, "Emmy's right. We need to talk to Harold before we do anything. We need to find out about the medallion, how it works, what kind of worlds it takes you to, and how to get home safely."

"I think Harold wants us to use the medallion to go somewhere, but I don't know where."

"Do you think it's Pangaea? Maybe that's why you had your vision. Maybe that's where we're supposed to go."

Silas said, "Just how bad were those volcanoes?"

Odo shrugged. "It doesn't matter how bad they were, because we're not going there. But just so you know, there were a zillion giant flaming molten hot lava rocks screaming down from the sky. Another few minutes and the massive clouds of burning hot volcanic ash would have buried everything, including me, just like what happened to Pompeii."

Sephie was silent. It wasn't so long ago that Odo had said there was absolutely no way he would ever visit the Land of the Dead, and a few days later they were on their way to find Charon the Ferryman on the River Styx, on a mission to bring Emmy's brother Jacob back from the Land of the Dead. "We need to go see Harold and we need to read his letter. Maybe we're not going to Pangaea, maybe it's the sunny beach Odo and I dreamed about."

Odo attempted a smile, but he was getting a bad feeling. He was pretty sure they weren't going to a sunny beach.

Chapter 13

Prince Nokk

The four friends took the bus to Odo's house after school, then headed down Asper Street to see Harold. Sephie had Stanley Livingstone's journal tucked under her arm. "The first thing we need to do is ask Harold if we can read the letter."

"Suppose he doesn't remember writing it?"

"Then we'll read it anyway. We don't have a choice, we have to find out what it says."

They ran up the front steps, Odo raising his hand to knock on the door. He stopped, slowly lowering his hand. "The door is open."

"Maybe Harold forgot to close it."

Odo pushed the door open a little farther, peering inside. "Harold? It's Odo Whitley. Are you there?"

There was no answer.

Emmy whispered, "I think I heard something."

"Harold? Are you home?"

"Maybe he's taking a nap."

"We should check on him. He could have fallen or

something."

Silas said, "Don't get mad, or think I'm a lunatic, but maybe whatever was eating the salmon, you know… did something… to Harold?"

"Are you saying a dinosaur ate Harold?"

"No, not exactly." Silas tilted his head. "I think I heard something in the kitchen, like plates rattling."

"Do you think something is eating Harold?"

"Stop saying that. That's not what I meant."

Sephie called out, "Harold? Are you there?"

Odo heard the refrigerator door slam shut.

The four of them peered around the corner into the sitting room.

Odo said, "The kitchen door is closed, but something is in there. Okay, here's the plan. On three, Silas runs over, flings open the door, runs into the kitchen and tackles whatever is eating the salmon."

"What? No, it could be Harold in there. I don't want to give him a heart attack or something. He's really old."

"Okay, creep over to the door and peek inside, then come back and tell us what you saw."

"Why don't you creep over and peek inside? It might not be Harold. It might be a pack of hungry velociraptors."

Four shrieks echoed through the house when the seven-foot tall dark blue lizard wearing red sweat pants and a Boston Red Sox tee shirt stepped out of the kitchen, an open can of tuna in its hand. Odo stumbled backwards, tripping over a chair, banging his elbow on the wall, sprawling across the floor. "What is that thing?"

The lizard creature turned, its eyes on Odo. "First day with the new legs?"

Odo blinked. "What?"

Sephie's voice was barely a whisper. "You can talk?"

The lizard gave them a pained look. "No, sorry, I can't talk. We could use sign language, though. Would that work for you? Maybe we could write little notes and pass them back and forth?"

The four friends looked at each other, then back at the lizard creature.

"Um… who are you, exactly?"

Silas said, "And where is our friend Harold?"

"You didn't eat him did you?"

The creature gave Odo a disgusted look, turning around and heading back into the kitchen, closing the door behind him.

Sephie said, "What was that thing?"

Odo whispered, "I only got a look at one of them, but I think it's one of the lizard people I saw in Pangaea, the ones who were escaping through the blue portal."

Silas said, "What's it doing here?"

"Eating Harold?"

"You need to seriously stop saying that. I was just joking. Sort of. But mostly joking."

"He had a can of tuna in his hand, not a can of Harold." Odo stepped over to the kitchen door, gently knocking on it. "Hello? Lizard person?"

The lizard called out, "The loopy old guy went for a walk. I didn't eat him."

The door swung open, the lizard scooping a clawful of tuna from the can, jamming it into his mouth. "You people really are something." He looked Odo up and down. "How come you're all pudgy and jiggly? You look like a jellyfish with legs."

Odo's face turned bright red. "Said the crazy lizard guy… um… eating tuna from a can."

"Ooh, you got me with that vicious barb, jellyfish."

"I'm not pudgy or jiggly. I've been lifting weights and I'm getting abs. Well, not exactly abs yet, but I'm gaining a lot of muscle mass. At least I don't eat tuna with my fingers. That's disgusting."

Emmy whispered, "Don't make him mad, Odo. He looks really strong."

The lizard strode past Odo to a six-foot wide mahogany table, picking it up with one hand, then setting it down. "How's that for abs, pudgy?"

Odo gulped.

Sephie smiled politely. "Do you happen to know when Harold will be back?"

"Not the slightest idea. Do you have any fresh fish? I'm starving. The insects here are abysmal, and so is this canned stuff. Back home you can feed a whole family on one dragonfly. Most people think the eyes are the best part, but I like the abdomen segments. Boil them up and slather on the sweet sauce. So good. Crispy crunchy on the outside, creamy and lumpy on the inside."

Odo's stomach was churning. "Are you trying to make me barf?"

Sephie heard the front door creak open, then slam shut.

"Harold? Is that you?"

Footsteps sounded in the hallway, Harold stepping into the room, a confused look on his face. "You're Odo, but who are you friends?"

"You've met them before, this is Sephie, Silas, and Emmy."

Harold gave the lizard an annoyed look. "The dinosaur is eating my tuna again. It's so annoying." He stepped over to the couch and took a seat, picking up a book. "The Triassic period was a very interesting time in Pangaea. Has anyone seen my medallion? I want to walk to Mars this afternoon, pick up a few rocks for my collection."

Odo took a deep breath, smiling at the lizard. "I think we got off to a bad start. I'm Odo Whitley, and these are my good friends Sephie, Silas, and Emmy. What's your name?"

"Are we besties now? How about a big group hug and then we can have cookies and a nice chat?"

"What is wrong with you? We're just trying to be nice, trying to make you feel welcome here."

"Nokk. My name is Nokk."

Harold called out, "He's Prince Nokk, the emperor's firstborn son."

"You're a prince?"

"Maybe."

Sephie said, "You're from Pangaea? I've read about the giant dragonflies they had back then."

"Giant *delicious* dragonflies they had back then."

"How did you get here? And how did you learn to speak our language?"

"I followed the loopy old guy here. I wanted to see where the jellyfish people came from. I was walking right behind him when all of sudden Pangaea was gone and I was in your weird little world. I picked up your language in about ten minutes from that plastic box over there."

Odo said, "It's called a radio. We have televisions and computers too, not just radios. We have lots of high tech stuff." Odo sucked in his stomach, trying not to look like a jellyfish.

Harold looked up from his book. "When I got back from Pangaea the dinosaur was here. He's very rude, probably from the late Triassic period."

Prince Nokk spun around, his eyes on Harold. "Again with the dinosaur? Really? The Varanian civilization has been around for two hundred thousand years. Our technology is beyond anything your tiny little human brains can possibly comprehend. I am *not* a dinosaur, I am a Varanian."

Odo grinned. This was good. "You do look a lot like a dinosaur, kind of a prehistoric lizardy look, late Triassic period, I'm guessing. "

Sephie glared at Odo. "What are you doing?"

"Nothing?"

Prince Nokk snorted. "Nice try, jellyfish. You're so *transparent*."

"Is that supposed to be funny? Why are you so rude?"

Sephie stepped between them, handing Harold the journal. "I read your dad's story. What an amazing adventure, finding an ancient Pangaean city under the ice in Antarctica."

Harold sat up when he saw the journal. "That reminds me, you have to take Prince Nokk back to Pangaea and send him through the portal to Varania."

Chapter 14

Consequences

Odo did not look pleased. "Why do we have to take him back? Can't he go back by himself? He's a big boy, he can lift tables with one hand."

Harold said, "The prince can explain."

Prince Nokk eyed Odo. "I'll use small words, if that helps."

Sephie put her hand on Odo's arm. "Don't let him get to you. He's a bully, just ignore it."

Odo gave a thin smile. "An alien dinosaur bully, the worst kind there is."

Prince Nokk pointed to a wide black watch on his wrist. "This is called a ConWatch. It tracks the long term consequences of your actions, and it's telling me that all four of you need to take me back to Pangaea so I can return to Varania through the portal in Emperia."

"What's Emperia?"

"The dome city in Pangaea."

Odo looked extremely dubious. "Sorry, a watch that tracks the consequences of your actions? That seems highly improbable. How does it work, and what happens if we don't take you back?"

"The watch is linked to the Temporal Quantum Event Tracking System, capable of processing three trillion septillion bits of information per millisecond across the known temporal spectrum. Not that time exists."

Odo blinked. "What does all that mean, exactly?"

Prince Nokk sniffed. "It means if I eat this can of tuna fish, my watch will tell me the future consequences of that action, and also what happens if I don't eat the tuna fish."

"How far into the future does it track events?"

"Roughly two hundred million years. If I'm about to do something that will have a negative impact on future events, my watch will beep, a warning appearing on the screen."

"You're saying if I eat an oatmeal cookie, it could somehow alter the universe a million years from now?"

"Precisely."

Silas whispered, "It's called the butterfly effect; it's a thing."

"How could your watch possibly know what's going to happen?"

"The Quantum Event Tracking System is the size of a small city, able to track a single chain of probabilities two hundred million years into the future. And it does it in four milliseconds."

Odo stared at Prince Nokk. "You're not just making

this up?"

"The Varanian civilization is two hundred thousand years old. Your civilization just discovered fire. What will your technology be like in two hundred thousand years?"

Odo said, "Fine, I give up, I was wrong. That's incredible."

Emmy asked, "What are the future consequences if we don't take you back through the portal?"

"Nothing drastic for the Varanians, but it's exceptionally bad news for Earth. There is a ninety-nine point seven six percent probability that an asteroid the size of your moon will pop out of the eleventh dimension traveling at half the speed of light and collide with your planet. Poof, goodbye little blue world."

"When would it happen?"

Prince Nokk tapped his watch. "Six months and four days from now."

Harold said, "You can use the medallion to go back to Pangaea and send him through the Emperian portal."

"I think we understand how to use the medallion, but we're not exactly sure how to get back again."

"Rotate the blue stone clockwise for three full turns. The stone will glow bright yellow and four seconds later you'll return to your original temporal and spatial point of departure. My father never knew what the medallion did. I didn't discover its true purpose until twenty-one years ago. Once you visualize your destination, you must keep walking. Walking tricks your mind into believing it's making a physical transition to another location."

"When I stopped walking, the beach world I was entering disappeared."

"Precisely. Once you're safely in the new world you don't have to worry about walking. You'll also be surrounded by an impervious energy shield for the first ten minutes or so. That's how I was able to walk on the moon without a space suit. All this is in the letter I wrote."

Prince Nokk had wandered back to the kitchen and was rummaging around in the cupboards. He held up a large jar. "What's this stuff?"

"It's called strawberry jam."

He twisted off the lid and smelled the jam, sticking his long black tongue into the jar, slurping jam into his mouth. "Not bad." He grabbed two more jars, stuffing them into the pockets of his sweatpants, finishing off the jar of strawberry jam.

Odo whispered, "So disgusting."

"What did you say, jellyfish?"

"I said I'm glad you like the jam."

Silas said, "Quick question. Why are you wearing sweatpants and a Boston Red Sox tee shirt?"

"Because it's freezing here, not toasty warm like Pangaea. I found them in the old guy's closet. They're a bit on the small side but I like the colors."

Odo said, "Why did you move to Pangaea?"

Prince Nokk shrugged. "We've colonized thousands

of worlds over the millennia. Pangaea is just one of them."

Odo said, "If you're the Emperor's firstborn son, why would they send you to a primitive little world like Earth filled with ferocious dinosaurs?"

Odo froze when he saw the dark anger appear on Prince Nokk's face.

Sephie saw it too, quickly changing the topic of conversation. "Harold, how do we know exactly when to arrive in Pangaea? Odo had a vision of people escaping through the blue portal, but we don't know exactly when it was."

Prince Nokk gave an annoyed groan.

Odo glared at him. "We're doing the best we can."

"Of course you are. You have my sincerest and deepest apologies. Please forgive me. How very rude of me."

Odo realized he was grinding his teeth.

Harold continued, "Just visualize the event and you'll arrive there. Replay your vision of Pangaea in your mind as you're walking."

"What about the giant volcanoes?"

"Excellent thought, perhaps you should arrive a few hours early. The energy shield will protect you, but only for about ten minutes."

Prince Nokk tapped his watch. "I'd like to get going sometime this week. Unless you'd rather discuss this for another few months?"

Odo forced himself to give a pleasant smile. "We need

to get our backpacks and some supplies. Just in case we need them."

"Get me some fish. And more of this jam. Even better, fish flavored strawberry jam. How good would that be on a boiled dragonfly abdomen? Yum."

Odo grabbed his stomach. "You need to stop that."

The four friends headed for the front door. "We'll be back in a couple of hours."

Odo called out, "Don't eat all Harold's tuna, dino boy."

Chapter 15

Not Even Close

As they stood outside Harold's house, Silas said, "What is with that crazy lizard? Why is he so rude?"

"Did you see the look on his face when I asked him why they sent him to a primitive planet like Earth?"

"He was seriously angry. No way did he want to go there."

"He's definitely hiding something. He could be lying about everything, including being the emperor's firstborn son."

"Maybe he's a crazy murder lizard. Maybe Emperia was an alien prison for super evil criminals and he escaped. Like in that movie, *Return of the Sinister Sorcerer.*"

"Emperia didn't look like a prison. It was a city with high tech vehicles and tall buildings and antigrav roads."

Emmy added, "If it was a prison they wouldn't have a big escape portal."

Silas said, "Good point. Prince Nokk is really angry about something. That's probably why he's so rude and sarcastic."

"I can't read his brainwaves. His brain isn't like ours, the mapping is different."

Odo snorted. "Can you believe he said I looked like a jellyfish with legs? How crazy is that?" He was carefully gauging Sephie's response.

Silas said, "That was actually kind of funny. Serious burn, pudge."

Sephie snickered. "It was a little funny, Odo. You don't look anything like a jellyfish though. Except for the translucent part."

"Thanks so much, I appreciate that."

"We'll meet back at Harold's house in two hours. Bring whatever you think we'll need."

Emmy gave a bright smile. "I think we have a few jars of strawberry fish jam at our house. I'll bring some in case Silas gets hungry."

"Barf."

"This is going to be so cool. I can't believe we're going to see dinosaurs. Real dinosaurs."

Odo said, "It's going to be a short trip. We send our rude lizard friend Prince Nokk through the portal and come straight home. Don't forget about the giant molten rocks falling from the sky, huge clawed lizards in the jungle, eight-inch long insects landing on you, and burning hot clouds of deadly toxic volcanic ash."

Silas laughed. "Sounds super fun. Can't wait."

Two hours later the four friends were standing in front

of Harold's house.

"Is everyone ready?"

"I brought binoculars and lots of snacks."

"Don't forget, we need to arrive a few hours before the volcanoes erupt."

"Got it. Two hours early."

Odo opened the front door, stepping inside. "We're back!"

Prince Nokk's voice echoed down the hallway. "Took you long enough."

Odo's jaw tightened. He couldn't wait to send Prince Nokk back through the portal. He was more annoying than Mike the Mechanic and his ridiculous three question challenges. He turned to Sephie, "Do you think there's a Mike the Mechanic on Earth? He said he existed simultaneously on tens of thousands of worlds."

"What made you think of him?"

"Because Prince Nokk is even more annoying than he is."

Sephie laughed. "I like Mike the Mechanic. He's really nice."

"Nice to you, not me. He's so annoying with his impossible three question challenges."

Prince Nokk hollered out from the living room. "Are we going or what? We're out of tuna fish and I'm starving. I could eat two dragonflies, eyes and all."

The friends stepped down the hallway into the main living room. Harold was sitting on the couch reading a tattered old magazine. He looked up at them. "Hello? Are you here about the dinosaur who's been eating my food?"

Odo glanced at Sephie.

She stepped over to Harold, putting her hand on his shoulder. "We are. The dinosaur is going to be gone soon and he won't be coming back. We'll make sure you have plenty of tuna fish."

"Wonderful, thank you so much. Is there anything you need?"

"We're all set, but thank you for asking. We'll be back in a few minutes."

"Lovely."

Odo said, "We need room to use the medallion. We'll have to go outside and walk on the sidewalk."

Silas eyed Prince Nokk. "Do you think anyone will notice a seven-foot tall lizard guy?"

"I am not a lizard guy and I'm not a dinosaur, I'm Prince Nokk of Varania."

"Sorry, that was rude."

Sephie grabbed a big blanket from behind the couch. "Put this over your head so no one can see you."

Emmy grabbed a pair of big rubber boots from the hallway. "These will hide your feet."

Prince Nokk studied the boots. "Is this really necessary?"

"People here are afraid of aliens, afraid of creatures that don't look like them. It's sad, but it's just the way it is here."

Prince Nokk pulled the boots on and draped the blanket over him. "I can't see anything."

Sephie took his hand. "I'll lead the way."

Odo glanced up and down the street. "All clear, I don't see anyone. Let's go."

They stepped out onto the sidewalk, Odo pulling the medallion from his pocket. "Here we go. I'm going to visualize the portal two hours before the volcanoes erupt. Everyone keep walking until this world is gone, completely replaced by Pangaea."

The group strolled down the sidewalk, Odo replaying the vision of Pangaea in his mind, visualizing the dense jungle and the huge transparent dome.

Sephie said, "Why is it getting foggy?"

"It's probably early morning fog in Pangaea. It's really humid there. That's good, it means we're arriving before the volcanoes erupt. We'll have plenty of time to send Prince Nokk through the portal."

Two minutes later they were enveloped in a dense fog. "I can't see anything. Does it seem really dark to you?"

"The sidewalk's gone, the ground is soft. I think we're there, but let's keep walking for another minute or two."

Sephie let out a shriek. "Stop! No one move!"

"What is it?"

Prince Nokk dropped the blanket onto the ground. He looked at the thick fog, then at his watch. "We're not even close to Emperia."

Sephie said, "Don't move, I think we're on the edge of a chasm."

"Everyone sit down, we need to wait until the fog lifts."

Prince Nokk studied his watch, "Emperia is almost a hundred miles from here on the other side of the chasm. The chasm is a fault line between the continents."

"Pangaea is breaking apart into the continents?"

Sephie said, "We know Emperia was in Antarctica, so this is probably Australia."

Odo said, "I've always wanted to visit Australia. Maybe we'll see some kangaroo dinosaurs."

"Not laughing."

As the fog lifted, Odo studied the sparsely vegetated desert that lay before them. "Why are we in a desert? I visualized Emperia exactly as I saw it."

"How are we going to cross that chasm?"

Chapter 16

Pliosaurus!

The sky began to brighten, the dense fog dissipating, Odo gazing down into the massive chasm. "It must be twenty miles across and it's filled with water. Look how big the waves are."

Silas said, "There was only one ocean back then, the Panthalassic Ocean. When Pangaea began breaking apart into separate continents the ocean poured in, filling the gaps between them. That water down there is the Panthalassic Ocean."

Odo said, "Truly fascinating, nerd, but how are we going to get across it?"

Silas turned to Emmy. "I think Dream Girl can help us with that."

Prince Nokk sniffed. "Is she going to build a boat out of sticks and sand?"

"Better than that." Emmy floated up into the air, smiling sweetly at Prince Nokk.

His jaw dropped. "You can fly? How? You have an antigravity belt?"

"I don't need one. I can change my physical body into a dream body and fly." She landed on the sand, taking Sephie's hand. "Everyone hold hands."

Prince Nokk was still staring at Emmy, an odd expression on his face. Odo took his hand.

Emmy said, "Is everyone ready? I'm going to make your physical bodies become part of my dream body. It's a strange sensation to be weightless, to have a non-physical dream body."

"We're all good. Take us up, Dream Girl." Silas turned to Prince Nokk, saying, "We call her Dream Girl because she can fly the same way you can fly in dreams."

The adventurers floated up above the desert, heading north across the massive chasm. Prince Nokk's eyes were wide. "You're certain we won't fall?"

"Not as long as we all hold hands."

Silas said, "Can we go down and take a look at the ocean? The waves look really cool. They're so big."

"Okay, just for a minute." They drifted down five hundred feet, Silas studying the huge crashing waves below them. "I think the waves are so big because of the narrow space that–"

Sephie let out a shriek when the monstrous long-necked creature shot up from the ocean, letting out a horrific roar, snapping its deadly jaws shut a few feet below them.

Prince Nokk screamed, "Up! Go up! Get us out of here!"

Silas cried out, "That was a pliosaurus! How amazing is that? Did you see how big it was?"

Prince Nokk shrieked, "What's wrong with you? Are you trying to kill us all?"

"What? I've never seen a pliosaurus before. Aren't they incredible? That one was forty feet long at least. Did you see the teeth on him? And those giant flippers?"

Emmy called out, "We've seen more than enough of the ocean. Next stop is Antarctica."

Ten minutes later they were flying a hundred feet above a dense rain forest. "That's a new world's record, we flew from Australia to Antarctica in under two minutes."

"Good one! What are those things flying toward us? They look like big birds."

Prince Nokk shouted, "Take us down! Those are pterosaurs! They'll kill us all!"

"They're pretty far away. They're kind of like the one in *Terrorsaurus*, but they're not as big and I bet they don't shoot beams of radioactive–"

"Down! We need to land now! Take us down!"

Emmy descended rapidly through the dense forest canopy, landing on the spongy jungle floor. Prince Nokk checked his watch, tapping it. He did not look happy.

Odo whispered loudly to Silas. "Someone doesn't like pterosaurs."

Prince Nokk glared at Odo. "I heard that. I'm not afraid of them, I was saving your lives. They are deadly dangerous creatures. I would suggest we walk to Emperia. The skies of Pangaea are not safe."

Odo said, "Hey, these are the same spiky trees I saw in my vision, the cycads, the trunks that look like giant pineapples."

Prince Nokk checked his watch, pointing toward a distant mountain range. "That way, about ninety-six miles."

"Ninety-six miles? Really?"

Sephie said, "Are you sure it's that far?"

"Someone did a less than satisfactory job of visualizing Emperia, but I won't name any names."

Odo shrugged. "I may have been thinking about the beach Sephie and I went to, gotten a little off track. It was so nice there. You know, all the white sand?"

"We're ninety-six miles off track, jellyfish."

"Can you please stop calling me that? I don't look anything like a jellyfish. In case you hadn't noticed, no one is calling you a dinosaur anymore, Prince of Varania."

Prince Nokk studied Odo. "Why are you solid?"

"I'm only translucent on Earth, not in other worlds. That's how it works."

Silas was studying the jungle. "I don't see any ghosts here."

"That's because people don't exist yet."

"Do you think dinosaurs have ghosts?"

"They do, but I can only see human ghosts. My grandpa said animals have ghosts, but I've never seen one."

Prince Nokk looked at them. "What are you people? Are you genetically engineered mutants?"

Sephie said, "We're the Odd Squad, four kids with cool powers who don't fit in."

"You don't fit in?"

"We're different from everyone else, but we found each other, and now we're best friends."

"What kind of powers do you have?"

"Emmy can fly, I'm translucent and can walk through walls, Sephie can see people's brainwaves and control their thoughts, and Silas can see ghosts, sometimes talk to them."

"No one in your world knows about these powers?"

"Only a couple of people; Wikerus Praevian, a Fortisian, and Mrs. Preke, a Plindorian formshifter. Other than that, we keep them a secret. If anyone else knew they'd probably kidnap us and try to control our powers."

"Or do weird experiments on us."

"Or think we were demons and try to kill us."

"Sephie can also shape physical objects using her mind."

"This is true?" Prince Nokk turned to Sephie.

She drew two symbols in the air, an open can of tuna fish appearing in her hand. "I visualize the object, creating a thought cloud, or energy field, then compress the energy into matter using my deeper self." She handed the tuna to Prince Nokk.

He sniffed at it, poking it with one claw. "This is physical matter, not Artificial Reality?"

"I don't know what that is."

"Interesting." Prince Nokk emptied the can of tuna into his mouth, swallowing it in one gulp. "Very good. Seems real."

Odo was about to remind him to chew his food, but there was something about Prince Nokk's expression that made him stop. It was a look he hadn't seen before.

Silas said, "Let's go, Odd Squad. We have to get to Emperia before the volcanoes erupt."

"How long until they erupt?"

Odo said, "I have no idea."

Prince Nokk checked his watch. "There is a ninety-nine point three percent probability they will erupt in twenty-nine days."

Chapter 17

Tourists

"Twenty-nine days? I guess I got here a bit early."

"The early bird catches the worm?"

"That would be great if we were looking for worms."

"Can we fly there?"

Prince Nokk pointed to six huge pterosaurs soaring high above the jungle.

"Right. I guess we walk."

"I don't like jungles, they're so hot and humid. Sweltering is the word I'd use. Or stifling, that works too." Odo stopped, pointing to something in the tree above him. "What is that?"

Silas said, "A really big striped snake?"

"Great, Pangaea has monster snakes. This is perfect." Odo pushed ahead through the thick undergrowth, heading toward the distant mountain range, keeping a wary eye on the branches above him.

Thirty minutes later he felt something thwack into his back. "Very funny, Silas. Nice try."

Sephie whispered, "Odo, it's not Silas, there's a really

big insect on your back."

"If this is a joke, it's not funny."

"It's not a joke, Odo. It jumped…it looks like a giant cockroach."

A searing wave of horror rolled through Odo, his legs suddenly wobbly. "Get it off me! Get it off!"

Prince Nokk strolled up behind Odo, grabbing the huge wriggling insect.

"What's happening? What are you doing?"

Sephie let out a horrified shriek.

Odo whipped around, facing the others. "Where is it?"

Sephie, Silas, and Emmy all had the same look of frozen horror on their faces. Silas was pointing mutely to Prince Nokk.

"Mmm, tasty."

Odo blinked. "Did you… did you…"

Sephie said, "I'm going to have nightmares forever, maybe longer."

Prince Nokk snorted. "What's the difference between eating an insect and eating a fish?"

Odo's mouth was hanging open.

Prince Nokk motioned for Odo to move. "Let's go. Do you mind if I walk behind you? Just in case? I'm still hungry, and I think the insects here are attracted to you."

Silas grinned. "It's probably his abs."

Odo ignored the comment, stopping at a thick tangle of gnarled vines. "Sephie, can you shape a machete so I can cut through these vines?"

She drew four symbols, a two-foot long machete appearing in a blink of blue light. "Is it too small?"

"It should work." He grabbed the machete, slicing through the vines. "Perfect, nice and sharp."

The adventurers forged onward through the steaming rain forest, Odo alert for sudden movements or sounds.

A few hours later they emerged from the jungle, Odo giving a loud groan when he saw the sprawling swampland in front of them. "This is worse than the jungle. We have to walk through a putrid stinky swamp? There's probably a million creepy things living in the muck."

"Tasty."

Odo turned to Prince Nokk. "Would you mind not talking about how tasty–" He abruptly ducked down, hissing, "Voices!"

They hunched down, peering out through the trees, Silas whispering, "I can see them."

"They look like big ants, but they're walking on two legs."

"And they're wearing clothes, carrying backpacks."

"The one in the front has a big yellow flag."

"Prince Nokk, do you know what they are?"

"I believe they are Tendorians, but I have no idea what they would be doing in Pangaea."

"Where are they from?"

"A few hundred light years away, a relatively advanced civilization, but nothing special about them that

I am aware of."

"What should we do?"

"We should talk to them." Prince Nokk stepped into the swamp, slogging through the muck toward the group of ant people, Odo and the others trailing behind him.

The Tendorians began chattering wildly when they spotted Prince Nokk, pulling flat silver disks from their pockets, lights flashing.

Odo ducked down. "Are those beam weapons? Are they shooting at us?"

Prince Nokk said, "They're taking pictures of us. They think I'm a dinosaur. They have no idea what you are."

"You can speak their language?"

"I have a universal communication implant that lets me speak fluently in all known languages. It's called a Unicom."

"You didn't learn our language listening to the radio?"

"Of course not."

"Why did you tell us you learned it from the–"

Prince Nokk called out, "I'm not a dinosaur. I'm a Varanian, and these creatures are time travelers from the future of this world."

As one, the Tendorians all tapped a small device on the side of their heads. The ant with the flag waved to them. "Hurry, get over here behind the trees, they're almost here! You're not safe out there! It's about to start!"

"They're speaking English. How is that possible?"

"Unicorn?"

"Oh, right."

The friends sloshed through the thick mud, quickly surrounded by the Tendorians, lights flashing. Two of them grabbed Odo, pushing him between them, resting their shiny chitinous arms on his shoulder. "Smile! Make a happy face!" One of them held out a silver disk, the flashing light nearly blinding Odo.

"Are you taking selfies?"

One of them poked Odo's stomach with a clawed foot. They both laughed, stepping back and taking a picture of him.

"What are you laughing at? I'm not pudgy. I've been working out."

Sephie pushed away from a group of Tendorians. "Enough pictures! No more, please."

Odo grinned. "Hey, Silas, that Tendorian looks just like my aunt. Get it, like my *aunt*?"

Sephie said, "Don't be rude, they're Tendorians, not ants."

"I know that, but it's funny because they look like–"

The Tendorian carrying the flag called out, "Attention! They'll be here any minute. This is the main battle, so get your cameras ready!"

Excited murmurs rippled through the group of Tendorians as they lined up on the edge of the swamp. One of them called out, "When do we get lunch?"

Odo whispered, "I'm confused. What is this?"

Silas said, "I think it's a tour group."

"A tour group? On Pangaea?"

"Kind of looks like it. The yellow flag, everyone walking behind the leader? All the cameras?"

One of the Tendorians gave an angry shout, pushing another one over into the goopy muck. "Out of the way, I can't see!"

The tour guide ran over to them. "No pushing! There will be plenty of time to take pictures. Please be considerate of others. Everyone will get a chance to see them. The battle lasts a full twenty-one minutes."

Odo said, "What battle? I don't see anything."

Silas' jaw dropped when the titanic Tyrannosaurus rex stepped out of the jungle into the swamp, it's enormous feet sinking down into the muck, making a horrid gloopy slurping sound.

"No way, a T-rex!"

"What's that in his mouth?"

"Half a dinosaur?"

"Eww."

Moments later the T-rex turned, a trio of heavily armored dinosaurs emerging from the jungle.

Chapter 18

Carnivore Wars

Silas let out a yelp. "Triceratops! Three of them!"

The T-rex let out a deafening roar, dropping the half eaten carcass into the muck. It turned to face the three triceratops, now circling slowly around him.

Odo said, "They look like tanks with horns. Really long, sharp horns."

Silas nodded. "Triceratops were a match for the T-rex. They're herbivores, but super strong, heavily armored, and dangerous."

The T-rex thundered toward one of the triceratops, brutally slashing at it with a powerful hind leg. One of the other triceratops charged the T-rex from behind, lowering its head, a deadly four-foot long horn raking across the T-rex's leg.

Sephie turned away. "I can't watch this. It's horrible."

Eighteen minutes later two of the triceratops were dead and the T-rex was badly wounded. The third triceratops was retreating, escaping into the jungle.

Odo stared in horror as the T-rex began eating one of

the triceratops. "This is bad. So bad."

The Tendorians were chattering wildly, their cameras flashing, some of them taking selfies against the nightmarish scenario behind them.

The guide called out, "Time to go! We're off to see the spinosaurus. The battle begins in twenty-four minutes!"

"When do we get lunch?"

"After the next battle."

"Who is the spinosaurus fighting?"

"A full grown bahariasaurus. You won't be disappointed."

Odo glanced up when he heard the humming noise above them. "It's an antigrav ship!"

The silver craft landed in front of them, a boarding ramp sliding out. "Everyone back in the ship!"

Odo ran over to the guide. "Can you take us to Emperia? We have to get there, it's really important, a matter of life and death."

"Emperia? Wrong tour, this is *Carnivore Wars*. Where's your guide?"

"We're not on a tour, and we have to get to Emperia or our planet will be destroyed by a giant asteroid."

The guide looked at his watch. "The spinosaurus battle is thirty-nine miles north of here. I can drop you off there and you'll avoid the swamp. That's as far as I go. We're on an extremely tight schedule. Next battle starts in twenty-one minutes. I'd lose my job if I took you there."

Silas asked, "How do you know when the dinosaurs are going to fight?"

The guide gave him a puzzled look. "I'm with Temporal Tours, time travel. I bring a group here almost every day. I've seen these same battles hundreds of times. We know exactly where they are, when they start, and how long they last."

"They're so violent."

The guide shrugged. "It's a brutal world. You coming with us or not?"

Odo nodded, the adventurers running up the ramp into the ship, taking their seats. Sephie was listening to a group of Tendorians describing in graphic detail the horrific battle they had just witnessed.

She whispered, "Why would anyone pay to see something like that? It's so horrible."

"They probably have tours where the dinosaurs don't fight."

"That would be fun. I'd love to see a brontosaurus. There's something about them I like."

"I'd like to ride one. That would be super fun."

The door hissed shut, the ship rising up above the forest canopy.

The guide called out, "Quetzalcoatlus on your right!"

"What's a quetzalcoatlus?" Odo looked out the window, his eyes on a monster pterosaur with a forty-foot wingspan soaring through the sky next to them.

"It's as big as a plane! That's the most incredible thing I've ever seen. Look how big his head is."

"I can't believe we're seeing dinosaurs."

Silas said, "Pterosaurs were flying reptiles, not dinosaurs."

Odo rolled his eyes, turning to Sephie. "Did Prince Nokk really eat that giant cockroach?"

She nodded, shivering. "Don't remind me. I keep seeing it in my mind. It was horrible. I wish I could unsee it. He just opened his mouth and swallowed it whole."

"Why did you tell me that? Now it's going to be stuck in my head."

"Sorry."

"He has an implant called a Unicom that lets him speak any language. He said when he's speaking it, it feels like the only language he's ever spoken. He didn't learn English from listening to Harold's radio, it was the Unicom."

"Why did he say he learned it from the radio?"

"I think he was trying to impress us. Like when he lifted that big table with one hand."

"People who show off are usually trying to get people to like them. I'm starting to think he's not what he seems to be. You saw how scared he was of the pterosaurs and the pliosaurus."

"He was shaking. I wonder why they sent him to Pangaea? He's definitely hiding something."

"He's also angry about something."

Odo nodded, glancing out the window. "Whoa! Look!"

Sephie leaned over, peering down at the terrain below. "A brontosaurus! There's a whole herd of them! Look how long their necks are."

"They must get really bad sore throats."

"Not listening, Odo. Too busy watching amazing dinosaurs."

"Check out that giant lake. It's probably an inlet from the ocean, not a lake."

"We're landing!"

The ship set down near the edge of the jungle, the adventurers stepping out next to a mammoth body of water, the Tendorians milling about, taking pictures of each other.

The guide called out, "Everyone stand behind those boulders. The spinosaurus will come out of the lake in nine minutes. The battle starts three minutes later when the bahariasaurus comes out of the jungle."

Silas studied an open grassy plain bordered by dense rain forests. "Crossing that plain will be a lot faster than going through the jungle."

"We'd better get going before the spinosaurus gets here. They are seriously scary."

"They live in the water? Do they have gills?"

Silas shook his head. "They breathe air, but they're super good swimmers, like crocodiles. They're huge, though. They have a big curved spiky spine on their back that looks kind of like a sail. It helps them to regulate their temperature. Dinosaurs were warm blooded, not cold blooded like reptiles."

Prince Nokk eyed the sparkling lake nervously. "We need to go if we're going to save your world."

Odo was pretty sure the only thing Prince Nokk was worried about was the deadly spinosaurus.

They headed off across the windswept plain, Prince Nokk glancing behind them every few minutes.

Silas said, "The spinosaurus spends most of its time in the water. It's not going to follow us. Besides, really big carnivores wouldn't eat us because we're too small."

Sephie poked Odo's stomach. "They might eat *one* of us."

Odo glared at her. "I'm not pudgy, I've been working out."

Emmy gave a shout. "There's the herd of brontosauruses! Next to the forest, they're eating leaves."

"Who knew you could get so big eating salad?" Odo frowned when no one laughed, their eyes on the herd of titanic long necked dinosaurs.

Silas studied the enormous creatures. "They're definitely Sauropods, but they're not brontosauruses. Most likely a diplodocus. It had a longer tail and neck, and wasn't as heavy as a brontosaurus. In fact, they think brontosaurus fossils may have been from a different sauropod that was incorrectly classified."

"Said the king of nerds."

Emmy called out, "There's a bunch of blue birds over that way! They're so cute, they look a little like big blue chickens."

Silas pulled a pair of binoculars from his pack, studying the feathered creatures. "Bad news, it's a pack of velociraptors. We have to leave now."

"They're not dinosaurs, they have big blue feathery tails and little wings. They're birds."

"A lot of dinosaurs had feathers, and these are velociraptors, voracious predators. We have to go hide in the forest. Now."

"They saw us!"

"Run!"

The friends took off across the grassy plain, racing toward the rain forest.

"They're coming after us! Hurry! They're fast!"

"Emmy, fly us out of here!"

Prince Nokk stopped, leaning over, gasping for breath. "It's happening. I can't stop it." He groaned, turning to face the rapidly approaching pack of vicious blue velociraptors. He grabbed his head, doubling over. "It hurts. It hurts! Make it stop!"

"Prince Nokk, we have to go! Emmy can fly us!"

The velociraptors were only a few hundred feet away when the air began to ripple in front of the prince, a wavering sphere of energy appearing, expanding rapidly with an eerie crackling sound. There was a blast of sizzling light, the thirty-foot wide orb flashing toward the pack of feathered carnivores.

When the radiant orb hit them, the velociraptors flickered and vanished. The massive sphere of energy shimmered with a pale blue green light, then faded to nothingness. Prince Nokk tumbled to the ground, lying motionless in the matted red grass.

Chapter 19

Prince Nokk's Secret

Odo kneeled down next to the prince. "He's breathing, I think he's okay."

"What was that? What did he do?"

"I don't know." Odo shook the prince's shoulder. "Prince Nokk? Are you okay?"

The prince made a gasping sound and sat up. He looked up at the others, a flicker of fear crossing his face. "Did you...you saw what I did?"

Sephie nodded. "What was that? What did you do to the velociraptors?"

The prince rose unsteadily, pressing his hands to his head. "It feels like there's a bright light in my head. It hurts when I try to fight it. I can't control it, it's too strong."

"You saved our lives. The velociraptors would have killed us."

Prince Nokk looked across the plain. "I haven't been completely honest with you."

"What do you mean? Honest about what?"

"I'm not what you think I am."

"You're not the emperor's son?"

"It's not that, I am his firstborn son, but there's something else."

Emmy said, "What did you do? How did you stop the velociraptors? What was that energy orb? Is it some kind of high tech weapon?"

The prince sighed. "When you said you didn't fit in with the others in your world, I understood what you meant."

"How?"

"I am much smaller and weaker than my brother and my father. My brother is younger, but he is a foot taller than I am, my father almost two feet taller. They used to call me Little Prince Nokky, people laughing at me behind my back. When I was younger the other students would make fun of me. The worst was Vork, a duke's son and a good friend of my brother Drakk. He would torment me whenever he got the chance. I don't know why he disliked me so much. Three years ago Vork challenged me to a fight in front of witnesses. He was a duke's son, so I couldn't back down; it would have brought great shame to my father."

"What happened?"

"It was the end of everything I knew."

"He beat you?"

"It was far worse than that. On the day of the fight over a hundred people had assembled on the palace grounds to watch. When I saw Vork step out of the crowd, I knew he meant to kill me. I could see it in his eyes. He would say it was an accident, not his fault, he hadn't realized how small and weak I was. I remember the cruel smile on his face. It was too much for me. That was the first time it happened. I lost control, I couldn't stop it. There was a blazing light in my head, I doubled over with the pain. I thought I was dying, then the orb flew out and Vork was gone."

"You killed him?"

"The punishment for murder on Varania is death, but my father intervened. He said I hadn't done it, he said he had irrefutable proof that a paid assassin from a neighboring province had fired a beam weapon at Vork, killing him. I was allowed to live because none of the witnesses dared to publicly dispute his story."

"That's why they sent you to Pangaea?"

"No. I was sent to Pangaea two years later when Vork reappeared on the palace grounds. He hadn't aged a day, and he had no idea where he'd been for two years."

Odo gave a puzzled look. "I don't understand. How is that possible? I thought you killed him?"

Sephie said, "You didn't kill him, you sent him to the future through a temporal wormhole."

"That is a crime worse than murder on Varania. Genetic engineering was outlawed over five hundred years ago. During the purge, all genetically altered Varanians were either imprisoned or put to death, all traces of the genetic engineering technology erased under penalty of death."

"They thought you were genetically engineered when you sent Vork to the future?"

"They said I was a mutant, that I had to die. My father couldn't cover up what I'd done, but he sent me to Pangaea in secret, announcing publicly that I had been put to death. It would have meant the end of his reign if they knew he had spared me. Even my brother Drakk doesn't know I'm alive. I'm an outcast, exiled from Varania."

Sephie gave him a sympathetic smile. "When I discovered I had powers, it terrified me. I thought I was going crazy. I had no idea why it was happening or how to control them. I found out later I was a Fortisian, that all Fortisians have powers and are taught how to use them as children. Odo and I have a good friend named Cyra, a Fortisian with incredible powers, much greater than mine. She trained me on Plindor. It took several months, but now I can control my powers and use them when I choose to."

Prince Nokk turned to Sephie. "Could you teach me how to control the orb?"

"I think so. You have an amazing gift, the ability to warp spacetime with your mind, sending someone through a temporal wormhole."

"Is that what I did?"

"I'm certain of it."

The prince slumped down on the grass. "Even if I

learn to control it, I'm still a mutant. They would put me to death if they found me."

"You're not a mutant, you're someone with an amazing gift who hasn't learned to control it. I also think you will use your power for good, not evil."

Prince Nokk studied Sephie's face. "I'm sorry for the things I may have said. Especially to you, Odo. I was so used to people making fun of me, laughing at how small I was, how weak I was, so I said things that—"

Odo shook his head. "Don't worry about it. Silas says rude things to me all the time and we're best friends."

Emmy said, "Can we call you Nokk instead of Prince Nokk?"

"I would like that. I would enjoy not being a prince."

"What did you mean when you said you were weak? You lifted that super heavy table at Harold's house with one hand."

"Another deception." Nokk held out his hand, displaying a large ruby red ring. "The ring has an antigrav beam in it. I wasn't lifting the table, the ring was."

Silas grinned. "I'm so weak I can barely carry a tune."

Odo clapped his hands, calling out, "Whoo hoo! Silas Ward takes the gold for the oldest and lamest joke in the universe!"

"What are you talking about? My grandpa told me that joke, it's a classic. It's always funny, like your face."

Nokk whipped around to see Odo's reaction.

Odo laughed. Sephie and Emmy were laughing too.

Odo was about to give a hilarious response when Silas whispered, "Ghosts!"

"What? Where?"

"A bunch of them near the sauropods. They look human."

"How could there be human ghosts here?"

"I don't know, but I'm going to find out."

The adventurers followed Silas as he headed toward the herd of mammoth dinosaurs, trying not to startle the huge creatures.

Sephie said, "Brontosauruses are so graceful with those long necks."

Silas shook his head. "It's not actually a brontosaurus, most likely it's a diplodocus. There were a lot of different kinds of sauropods, the biggest was the titanosaur, over one hundred and–"

"I'm going to call him Bronto. Odo, you should try to ride it."

Odo eyed the titanic slow moving creature as it stripped the leaves off a tall tree. "Maybe later."

Silas headed over to the group of ghosts. They were definitely human, but their clothes were from a variety of eras, some current, some futuristic, some distinctively old fashioned. Silas sent out a thought.

"How can you be here when people don't exist yet?"

Half a dozen of the ghosts turned, looking at Silas.

"Said the human standing next to a dinosaur."

Silas could hear the ghosts roar with laughter.

"Right, I get that, but seriously, how can you be here?"

"Where should we be? Haunting an old house? Maybe an abandoned amusement park? Scaring away nosy teenagers?"

There were peals of laughter, louder this time.

One of the ghosts drifted over to Silas.

"Not many people can see us."

"My grandpa and I can both see ghosts."

"Interesting. I was a physicist in the early 1900s. I've learned a lot since I moved on to this form. Did you know objects without mass can cross all dimensions, travel anywhere in time? Not that time exists, of course. That's how we can be here, our spectral bodies don't have any physical mass."

"You're a time traveling ghost?"

"A temporal tourist, a student of the universe. During their time on Earth, everyone here dreamed of one day seeing the dinosaurs. And here we are, our wishes come true. We can go anywhere we want; to other worlds, other dimensions, anywhere. I spent four years in ancient Rome during the reign of Augustus, the first emperor. Very interesting time. Augustus was a fascinating person, quite brilliant."

"Can you visit the future?"

"I can visit as many futures as I want."

"What does that mean, as many futures as you want?"

"It's complicated, but there isn't just one future, there

are many."

"We're trying to get to Emperia so we can stop a giant asteroid from destroying Earth. Is there a quick way to get there?"

The ghost smiled.

"What? Why are you smiling?"

"I could tell you why, but it would spoil your grand adventure. That's what life is, you know, a grand adventure. Never knowing what's going to happen next. All part of the fun."

"Right. Well, have fun watching the dinosaurs. There's a big spinosaurus about ten miles to the south if you're interested. They're really amazing."

"Wonderful, thanks. Have fun in Emperia. And anywhere else you might be going." The ghost gave a broad theatrical wink.

"Why did you wink?"

"I didn't wink, I had something in my eye."

"You're a ghost, you don't have eyes."

The ghost laughed. *"Clever. Safe travels, my friend. Enjoy your adventure."*

Odo called out, "Are you talking to the ghosts? What did they say?"

"They're time traveling ghost tourists who like dinosaurs."

"Think how much money they save on hotels and transportation."

Silas stared at Odo. "Sephie's right, something is

wrong with your brain."

Chapter 20

The Stranger

Odo strolled along next to Nokk, his eyes on a huge birdlike creature running in and out of the rainforest. "That's a monster big bird. Twice as big as an ostrich and it has that super scary looking beak."

Silas said, "Those are called Terror Birds, and there were lots of different kinds of them. They look scary, but they're herbivores. They use their big beaks to grind up seeds and–"

Odo stopped in his tracks, running to the edge of the forest.

"Look what I found!"

Silas and Sephie darted over him, their eyes on the twelve-foot wide nest made of branches and leaves. "Are those eggs?"

"Dinosaur eggs. Big ones, maybe a T-rex. Or a quetzalcoatlus." Odo pushed aside some damp moss, touching one of the elongated eggs. "It's soft, not hard, kind of leathery."

"We need to go, the mom might be around."

"I could bring an egg home with us. How amazing would that be?"

Sephie said, "I want you to imagine something, Odo. Can you do that?"

"What do you want me to imagine?"

"I want you to imagine the look on your dad's face when a six-foot tall baby T-rex smashes your bedroom door open and comes downstairs hunting for a snack while your dad's having his breakfast."

"I see where you're going with this. I'll just leave the eggs here."

"I never wanted to be a prince."

Odo turned to Nokk. "What?"

"I never wanted to be a prince. I like science, engineering, technology, inventing new things. I built this antigrav ring."

"That's so cool. Silas is really good at all that stuff. His grandpa is an amazing inventor."

"I didn't really invent anything new, the ring was just a novel application of existing technology."

"It's still cool. People in our time would pay a jillion dollars for a ring like that."

"Primitive cultures always misuse advanced technology. We have very strict laws about sharing our tech with less advanced civilizations."

"I get that. Silas' grandpa knows a lot about alien technology and he keeps it all secret. He said people would use it to make more powerful weapons and start wars. The last thing our world needs is more wars."

"Exactly."

"Has your ConWatch warned you about anything?"

"I disabled the warnings. They're very annoying. They make us wear the watches, but I don't like them. They can track us with them. The watch told me not to follow Harold, but I did it anyway. I wanted to see where he was going. I was curious."

"What did your ConWatch say would happen?"

"Something about a terrible plague in some other dimension. I didn't pay much attention to it."

"It really does sound annoying. I wouldn't want to have a machine telling me what to do every ten minutes. That's what parents are for."

Odo waited for Nokk's laugh, but it didn't come. He wasn't smiling. "I've been told what to do and what to say my whole life. No more."

Sephie was listening to Odo and Nokk as they strolled along, but she was also studying a strange glow at the edge of the forest a hundred feet ahead of them. There was someone there, and their brainwave pattern was similar to Nokk's.

"Can we stop for a minute?"

"What's wrong?"

"I think there's a Varanian hiding in the trees up ahead. I think they're watching us. I can see their brainwaves."

Nokk gave a start. "What do they look like? Are they

wearing gray uniforms?"

"I can only see their brainwaves. It's just one person."

"That's good news. If it was Friends of Varania there would be a group of them. They never travel alone."

"Who are the Friends of Varania?"

"It's a very old organization, originally created to help people, to make sure all citizens had everything they needed, but they've changed over the last hundred years. People are afraid of them now."

"Do you think they're looking for you?"

"I don't know. I came to Pangaea with a new name and false records, but FOV has eyes everywhere, even in the royal palace."

"Let's go find out who it is. I'm getting a feeling."

They followed Sephie as she headed toward the spot where the Varanian was concealed.

As they approached, Sephie called out, "Hello! Do you need help? Are you okay?"

A Varanian wearing a dark blue jumpsuit stepped out, a glowing green cylinder in one hand. It was pointed directly at Sephie.

Nokk hollered, "Beam gun!"

The Varanian studied them. "Who are you, and why are you here? No one is supposed to be this far from Emperia. It's dangerous out here." The Varanian's eyes scanned Nokk's Boston Red Sox tee shirt. "What are you wearing? What is that? Where is your uniform? Who are these creatures?"

"That's a lot of questions."

The beam weapon was now pointed at Nokk. "So give me a lot of answers."

"The short story is I disobeyed my ConWatch and followed a time traveler back to their world. That's where I got these clothes. I was cold and I was trying to fit in."

"How did that work out?"

"Not very well, I'm afraid. I had to wear a blanket over my head."

"You disobeyed your ConWatch? That's a serious crime."

"There are going to be massive volcanic eruptions and earthquakes in the next few weeks. Emperia is doomed. Many will escape through the portal back to Varania, but some will stay here and live with the dinosaurs."

"You're going back to Varania? After disobeying your ConWatch?"

"The ConWatch said if I don't go through the portal, Earth will be destroyed by a massive asteroid a hundred and fifty million years from now."

The Varanian studied the others. "These creatures are from that time?"

"Yes, far in the future. The dinosaurs die out, mammals evolve, humans become the primary life form."

"They look kind of puny to be a primary life form."

Odo's jaw tightened.

"These ones are different, they have powers." He turned to Emmy. "Show her."

139

Emmy floated up ten feet above the ground.

The Varanian gave a start. "They're mutants? Genetically engineered?"

"Only Odo. He's a translucent. He can walk through walls."

"What can the others do?"

"Sephie is half Fortisian and can read brainwaves, shape objects, and manipulate thoughts, memories. Silas can see ghosts and talk to them."

The Varanian was silent for a moment, then said. "A very impressive set of skills. They could prove useful."

"What do you mean?"

"Why did you disobey your ConWatch? That's a serious crime with serious consequences."

"I wanted to see where the time traveler came from. I was curious."

"Curiosity can be more dangerous than disobeying your ConWatch."

"You haven't told us who you are, what you're doing out here by yourself."

"You're right, I haven't told you."

"Are you going to?"

"Not yet. Not until I know more about you. I have a camp in the woods. You'll be safe there. We can talk."

Odo said, "What kind of camp?"

"A nice one. Follow me." The Varanian turned, heading into the forest.

Odo whispered to Nokk, "What do you think?"

Nokk had an odd look on his face. "I think she's the most beautiful girl I've ever seen."

"That's a girl?"

Nokk gave him a surprised look. "Of course she is. How could you not see that?"

"I… um… wasn't really paying attention to what she looked like?"

Odo stopped when he stepped through the trees and saw the fifty-foot wide silver dome. "Whoa. Not what I was expecting. Pretty fancy tent."

Nokk's jaw dropped. "She's an AR engineer."

Chapter 21

Elia

The Varanian girl tapped a wide iridescent wristband, a doorway appearing in the dome. She motioned for the others to enter.

Odo stepped inside. "It's like a one way mirror, I can see through the walls. This is amazing. How did you get all this stuff? The dome is huge."

Nokk said, "She's an AR engineer."

"Right, but what does that mean exactly?"

"Artificial Reality. That's what she does."

The girl smiled at Odo. "My name is Elia. I moved to Pangaea almost a year ago."

"You brought all this stuff with you?"

"No, it was created using Artificial Reality." She tapped her wrist, the dome and all its contents vanishing, Odo suddenly standing on the spongy jungle floor. She tapped her wristband again and the dome reappeared. "It takes many years of training to become a proficient AR engineer. I started when I was a child. The wristband is linked to my mind, and my thoughts must be absolutely clear, precisely focused."

Odo stepped over to one of the chairs, touching it. "It's real. It's solid."

Elia tapped her wrist and the chair vanished. "It's not real, it only seems real." She stepped over to a table, a pale yellow fruit resembling a large apple blinking into view, a silver knife next to it. She motioned for Odo to approach. "Pick up the bolyfruit."

Odo picked it up, smelling it. "Smells kind of good. It's heavy."

"It's AR, not real. It's a hollow shell with a gravitational force multiplier so it feels heavy, has weight."

"This is hollow?"

"Try cutting it in half with the knife."

Odo sliced the bolyfruit in half. "It's not hollow." He held up half the fruit, showing it to her.

"It's still hollow, but now there are two hollow shells instead of one. If you keep cutting it in half you'll simply be increasing the number of hollow shells. You could eat the fruit and it would seem real, but it would have no nutritional value. It's composed of incredibly thin layers of energetic fields. I created the bolyfruit using low energy AR. That's why you were able to cut it with the knife." She tapped her wrist, the pieces of fruit and the knife vanishing.

Sephie said, "Elia, our friend's father discovered the remains of Emperia during our time. It was hidden beneath an ice sheet that covers Antarctica. He called some of the buildings ghost buildings, said he could put his hand through them like they weren't there. Were they built using AR?"

"They were built with high energy AR, which lasts a very long time, but it slowly fades away, the energy ribbons dissipating. In time the AR objects just fade away."

"All the buildings in Emperia are AR buildings?"

"As are the buildings on Varania. There are a few ancient cities that are not AR, considered by some to be sacred sites."

Silas said, "AR is like the virtual reality on my computer, but it's out in the real world. You can manipulate it any way you want?"

Elia stepped over to a wall, pressing her hand against it. A doorway appeared, opening to a new room filled with furniture. "You can add a room whenever you want, change whatever you want."

"That's incredible."

"It's just science, just physics, the manipulation of energy. Nothing more, nothing less."

Odo said, "It's still incredible. That would be so cool to have that in our world. Your world must be amazing."

"Not as amazing as you might think. Technology changes, but people don't."

"What do you mean?"

"Our technology is far more advanced than yours, but our world is far from a paradise. We face the same challenges as your world. Technology does not eliminate insatiable greed and the endless lust for power. It does not bring an end to evil, ignorance, and fear, to the dreadful darkness found in some people."

Sephie nodded. "Sometimes I forget."

Odo said, "Nokk, you should tell Elia about your power."

Nokk gave Odo a sharp look. "It's nothing, it's not a power."

"Seriously? It's an incredible power. Nokk can send people to the future through a temporal wormhole."

Elia spun around, the beam weapon appearing in her hand, aimed at Nokk. "I've only heard of one person who could do that. They told us you were dead, Prince Nokk."

Odo felt sick. "Sorry, I was just... I didn't think..."

"My father sent me to Pangaea. They were going to kill me for being a mutant. He gave me a new name and history. If anyone finds me, I'm dead. Sephie is teaching me to control my power."

Elia lowered the weapon slightly. "What will you do when you get back to Varania? Return to the royal palace?"

"I'll never go back there. I'll keep hidden until I can escape to another world. One where people are free to do what they want, a world without ConWatches, where mutants can live without fear."

Elia took a seat, tapping her fingers on the arm of her chair. Finally she looked at Nokk, saying, "You are not like your father?"

Nokk shook his head. "I am nothing like him at all."

"There are people who wish him ill. What do you think about that?"

"He is a harsh ruler who has made many enemies. Having enemies is a price he is willing to pay. It is not a price I would pay."

Elia studied Nokk's eyes, her face softening. "I have a secret."

Nokk looked at her curiously. "What kind of secret?"

"A secret known only to a handful of people on Varania, your father being one of them. That is why he has ordered the Friends of Varania to kill me on sight. He wants me dead because what I discovered could end his reign and change life forever on Varania."

"My father wants to kill you? I don't understand. Are you sure?"

"I am more than certain. Three times the Friends of Varania have tracked me down and tried to assassinate me, and three times I have eluded them using AR. That's why I'm here hiding in the jungles of Pangaea."

Odo said, "What did you discover? What is the emperor afraid of?"

"I can't tell you. To know the secret is to put your life in great jeopardy."

Nokk took a seat across from Elia, looking at her curiously. "You said if your secret was revealed it would change life on Varania forever. How would life change?"

"People would live their own lives, follow their own

destinies, become whatever they want to be. There would be no more ConWatches."

"That would happen if you revealed your secret?"

"It's far more complicated than that, and I can't do it by myself. It's a dream, it's never going to happen."

Nokk studied her face. "Suppose you had help from someone who could send people to the future?"

Emmy said, "Or someone who could fly?"

"Or someone who could manipulate thoughts and memories."

"Or someone who could walk through walls."

Elia blinked. "You are willing to help me? You would be risking your lives. It's so much more dangerous than you can imagine."

Nokk said, "I have been told what to say and what to do my whole life. That needs to end, not just for me, but for all Varanians."

Elia said, "I need to think about this. People could die."

Sephie said, "If I'm going to help, I'll need to understand how Varanian brains function so I can manipulate their thoughts and memories."

Elia tapped her wristband, a three-foot long brain appearing, hovering in front of Sephie. "This is an AR model of a living Varanian brain. Touch any part of it and its function will be revealed. Ask it to display any emotion or memory, and the corresponding areas of the brain will light up. It's a living three dimensional AR Varanian brain map."

Sephie grinned. "This is exactly what I need, but it will take me four or five days to fully understand the various neural functions and pathways."

Nokk said, "I'm going to practice my power until I can send a person or an object to a precise moment in time."

Elia said, "If you send someone to the future, can you bring them back to the present?"

"I don't know. It might be possible if I created a reverse temporal wormhole in the future. Perhaps they could step through it and return to the present. I don't want to try it until I have a better understanding of my powers."

Elia said, "You're certain you want to help? All of you?"

Sephie said, "We are."

Elia nodded. "You have my deepest gratitude. I will work on a plan while you are making your preparations."

"Don't forget about the volcanoes. They erupt sometime in the next three weeks."

"That will work to our advantage. The chaos created by the erupting volcanoes will allow us to pass through the portal unnoticed."

Odo said, "In my vision there were hundreds of vehicles going through the portal at the same time."

"This is useful information. When the time comes I will use AR to create an unregistered antigrav car to carry us through the portal."

Emmy said, "What happens when we get to Varania?"

Elia shook her head. "I don't know."

Chapter 22

Emperia

"One minute left." Odo's eyes were focused on the table in front of him. Sixty seconds later a bolyfruit blinked into existence.

"Perfect, you sent it exactly three minutes into the future, almost to the second."

Nokk smiled. "I understand how to gauge the time now. It's much easier than I thought it would be, but I couldn't have done this without Sephie's help."

"She learned a lot from our Fortisian friend Cyra."

"How far into the future can you send someone?"

"I don't really know."

"It would be fun to see what the world is like five hundred years from now. All the new technology would be amazing."

Sephie put her hand on Odo's shoulder. "But not so amazing if you got stuck there and couldn't get back. Especially if the world had been invaded by giant poisonous alien spiders."

"Why would you say that?"

Emmy added, "Or by huge Terrorsaurs that shoot radioactive beams out of their mouth."

Odo rolled his eyes. "Ha ha."

Two weeks had passed, Sephie training Nokk in the morning and studying the Varanian brain map in the afternoon. Nokk spent most of his spare time sending out time orbs faster and faster until it had become almost a reflex.

Sephie called out, "Nokk, I need your help."

Nokk stepped over to Sephie. "What do you need me to do?"

Sephie handed him a small stone. "Hold this stone, but don't tell me which hand it's in."

He took the stone, putting his hands behind his back. "Done."

"Is it in your left hand?"

"No."

Sephie watched his prefrontal and parietal cortex flare brightly. "You're lying."

"Correct."

"Let's try it again."

Half an hour later Sephie had not been wrong once.

"Okay, now I want you to look around the room and tell me if you see anything different, anything odd."

Nokk scanned the room, his eyes widening. "There is a very small T-rex walking toward me."

"Excellent. Look at Odo. What do you see?"

Nokk laughed. "There is a pterosaur sitting on his

head eating a yellow bolyfruit."

"Perfect, I can manipulate your visual cortex. I'm going to give you a false memory now. Tell me what it is."

Nokk glanced over at Elia, currently seated in front of a pulsating white orb. He whispered to Sephie, "Elia told me how handsome I was. That's the memory. It's so clear."

"Excellent." Sephie didn't mention she had read Elia's brain waves while Nokk was talking to her. Elia liked him, but she was also very angry at him. Sephie had no idea why.

Emmy leaned in through the doorway, calling out, "Come outside, I want to show you something."

They stepped out of the dome, spotting Emmy standing next to a massive five-foot tall granite boulder.

Elia said, "Where did that rock come from?"

Emmy feigned surprise. "Oh, there it is! I was wondering where I put that." She wrapped her arms around the rock and floated up into the air.

Silas' jaw dropped. "How are you doing that?"

"The same way I fly you guys around. If I make the rock be part of my dream body, it loses its physical mass. Check this out." She flew the rock fifty feet up, then released it. The friends watched as it plummeted to the ground, landing with an earthshaking thud, embedded deeply in the forest floor.

"I don't know why I didn't think of this before."

"That's amazing."

Elia said, "A very useful power."

Sephie said, "I think we're ready. Nokk can control his temporal wormholes, and I've learned everything I need to know about Varanian brain mapping."

Silas grinned, "And Dream Girl can lift giant rocks."

Odo woke the next morning dreaming that his mom was shaking him, trying to wake him. "Trying to sleep. Five more minutes."

Sephie shook his arm again. "Odo! Earthquake! Wake up!"

Odo jumped out of bed, Silas calling out, "There's a big plume of black ash to the south! The volcanoes are erupting! It's happening!"

Elia raced outside, tapping her wristband, the dome and its contents vanishing. She ran two fingers across the rectangular screen, then tapped it, a twenty-foot long silver craft appearing in front of them.

Odo said, "Can I fly it?"

Elia laughed, hopping into the craft, pressing a series of glowing tabs. "Not today, rush hour traffic is going to be brutal."

The others climbed in, gray safety harnesses snaking around them, the silver ship humming. Silas had a huge grin. "This is so cool. I love antigrav ships."

Odo gave a start when a clear canopy appeared above them. "Where did that come from?"

"AR. We can see out, but they can't see in, a security measure in case there are cameras at the portal entrance."

The ship hummed, rising up above the treetops.

"Whoa, check out those volcanoes!"

"Look at the lava and rocks shooting up! Those ash clouds are crazy, they look solid, like a giant black wall."

Emmy hollered out, "There's a big crack in the ground! The trees are falling into it!"

Elia said, "We don't have much time." The ship shot forward, Odo pressed back against his seat.

Silas called out, "Look at all the ships heading for Emperia!"

"Is that giant dome Emperia?"

"That's it. They've opened it up for the ships."

"The city is huge. I can't imagine what Harold's dad thought when he found it in Antarctica."

Elia studied the antigrav car's display screen, eyeing a blinking violet light. "We're good to go. Hang on."

Odo screeched when they swerved into the stream of vehicles streaking toward the portal. He watched as two ships collided, one spinning down into the jungle, exploding in a raging ball of green fire.

"We're almost there!"

Elia dropped the ship down, now only a hundred feet above the ground, the massive dome city directly ahead of them. A dark blue ship bumped into them, Elia yanking a manual control knob, keeping them on course.

"There's the portal!"

"Got it! Here we go!"

Five seconds later the adventurers shot into the dome

at over a hundred miles an hour, Odo closing his eyes as they flashed through the huge shimmering blue portal.

Chapter 23

Varania

Odo opened his eyes, gaping at the vast sprawling city that lay before them, the skies above it filled with hundreds of ships streaming out of the portal. "How tall are those buildings?"

Elia said, "That blue one is over a mile tall. Most of the others are under a mile."

"How is that possible? They're so narrow, why don't they fall over?"

"They have no physical mass, they're created using high energy AR. They're not affected by wind or gravity. They're inexpensive to build and easy to update and remodel, just like my dome in Pangaea."

"Do most people live in the city, or just work there?"

"Almost everyone uses AR clonal avatars and works from home. Some of the older people like to go in person, but not many."

"They all wear ConWatches?"

"They have no choice, it's a mandate from the emperor. To disobey it is a serious crime."

Silas said, "Where do we go from here? What happens if people recognize Nokk?"

"They won't get the chance. We're leaving the city as quickly as possible, before Friends of Varania spot our unregistered ship. That would be a most unfortunate turn of events." Elia made a sharp banking curve, streaking across the city.

Half an hour later Odo said, "Look at all the farms down there. It looks almost like Earth, except the plants are all red."

Elia said, "My grandpa's old summer house is out here. We can stay there for now. The family still owns it but no one goes there. It's rustic. Once we get there we can formulate a plan to–"

Odo called out, "I think we're going down. How come we're going down?"

Emmy cried, "There's a ship behind us with flashing orange lights!"

Elia groaned. "Friends of Varania! They've taken control of our ship, forcing us down."

"What are were going to do?"

"I'll think of something. I can use AR. When we land I'll get out, but you stay in the ship and keep hidden. If they see you they'll ask questions. There are lots of aliens on Varania, but no humans."

The ship touched down next to an open field lined with long rows of tall leafy red plants, the Friends of Varania ship landing behind them. Elia climbed out, giving a friendly wave. Four gray suited FOV agents emerged from the ship, one of them carrying a short deadly weapon.

Elia said, "Is something wrong? Was I going too fast?" Her fingers were casually resting on her wrist band.

The agents approached her, one of them scanning the antigrav car with a small black device.

"Your ConWatch has been deactivated and you're driving an unregistered vehicle. You'll need to come with us." He turned to the others, saying, "Five life forms in the ship, one Varanian, four unknown alien."

The agents pulled out weapons, aiming them at the ship.

The first FOV agent hollered, "Everyone step out of the ship, hands in the air. Now!"

Silas whispered, "What should we do?"

The first agent abruptly holstered his weapon, his eyes on Elia.

"Please forgive me, I didn't recognize you, Princess Odo. You have my deepest apologies. Is there anything we can do to assist you?"

Elia knew instantly that Sephie was manipulating the agent's thoughts. She glared at him. "You can make certain this never happens again or I guarantee the emperor will hear about it."

"Of course, Princess Odo. Again, you have my deepest apologies." The agents slowly backed away, returning to their ship, departing moments later.

Elia darted back to the ship. "Well done, Sephie!"

"They won't remember any of this, I wiped their memories. We're safe for now."

Odo glared at Sephie. "Princess Odo? Really?"

"It's all I could think of. Your name just popped into my head."

Silas snickered. "Princess Odo. I like it."

Emmy said, "You were the first person she thought of, Odo. That's a good thing."

"That's true. At least she wasn't thinking about the guy who asked her to the dance."

"You need to let that go."

"Sorry. Thanks for saving us. You can borrow my tiara any time you want."

Sephie punched his arm. "I'll wear it to the next dance."

Elia hopped into the pilot seat, tapping the controls, the ship soaring up a hundred feet. "It will take us half an hour to reach my grandpa's summer house. Keep an eye out for the Friends of Varania."

It was Silas who spotted the group of ships heading toward them, their orange lights flashing. "Friends of Varania! Five ships!"

Sephie said, "How did they find us? I erased their memories."

"It must have been recorded on their cameras."

Elia said, "I have a plan. I'm putting the ship into a

spin and taking us down fast. As soon as we land, jump out and run, find a place to hide. I'll catch up to you."

Odo gave a yelp when the ship started spinning wildly, dropping like a stone. "What are you going to–"

Ten seconds later the ship hit the ground, landing with a jarring thud between the long rows of tall dark red plants.

"Out! Now!"

The friends leaped out of the ship, running off into the field, hiding under the broad red leaves. Elia tapped her wristband, the ship twisting into a tangled mass of jagged metal and shattered glass, a huge ball of roiling green fire erupting from the wreckage. She raced after them, ducking under the plants. "Shh! Keep still!"

The five FOV ships arrived a minute later, hovering silently over the raging fire. A beam of blue light shot down from one of the ships, moving slowly across the wreckage. The orange flashing lights blinked off, the ships turning away, heading east.

Emmy whispered, "You did it."

"I created six AR bodies in the ship, just in case they scanned it. It's a good thing they didn't know they were chasing an AR engineer. They wouldn't have left so quickly."

"Where are we?"

"I'm not exactly sure. Maybe ten miles from Grandpa's house?"

"Can you check your ConWatch?"

"I shut it off using AR so they can't track me. It won't take them long to identify me using facial recognition on the recorded images."

"Which way?"

"Toward that mountain."

They crept through the fields, keeping low, Sephie peering through the leaves at a farmhouse ahead of them. "Keep down, there's someone in the yard. It looks like a kid."

Odo studied the young Varanian sitting under a wide leafy tree. "What's he doing?"

They watched as he moved his hand slowly back and forth, a red plant emerging from the ground. Less than ten seconds later it was two feet tall, covered with round yellow fruit the size of strawberries. He plucked one off and ate it.

"Whoa, how is he doing that? Do plants grow that fast here?"

Elia shook her head. "They do not. He's far too young to be an AR engineer, and that leaves only one possibility. He's a genetically engineered mutant."

Chapter 24

Lightning

The young Varanian gave a start when he saw the group of adventurers step out of the field. He jumped up and ran into the farmhouse. Seconds later a tall Varanian farmer wearing well worn clothes emerged, a long gray cylinder in his hands. He did not look friendly.

Nokk waved to him, his eyes on the farmer's antiquated beam rifle. It was old, but still deadly. "Hi, there, could you possibly help us? We're trying to find my friend's house. It's around here somewhere, but we're lost."

The farmer walked toward them, his weapon still pointed at them. "I know you saw him."

"He's your son?"

"I can't let you turn him in to the Friends of Varania."

"He's a mutant?"

"I don't like that word. His name is Din. He's not a mutant, he's my son."

Emmy floated up into the air. "I don't like that word either."

The farmer stared at her, lowering his weapon slightly. "Who are you?"

"I'm Emmy, and these are my friends. We all have powers."

Elia said, "The FOV is after us. We crash landed our ship, made it look like we all perished. I'm trying to find my grandpa's old house so we can hide from them."

The farmer studied her face. "You can hide in the barn for now. Drones are patrolling the area, looking for mutants and anyone not wearing ConWatches."

"I shut mine off."

"How?"

"I'm an AR engineer."

The farmer stared at her. "Never met one before. Show me. Prove it."

Elia tapped her wrist and a long wooden handled steel shovel appeared in front of her. "You can have it. It will last for a few thousand years."

The farmer took the shovel, examining it. "Thanks, I could use a good sturdy shovel. Follow me."

They headed over to the dilapidated wooden barn, the ancient rusty hinges creaking as the farmer pulled the doors open. "You can stay in here."

Elia said, "This barn is made from real wood, not AR?"

"My father and I built it. Needs some paint is all."

"I could make you a new AR barn."

"FOV would be here in a minute when their drones

saw it."

"Good point."

"You hungry?"

Odo nodded.

"Stay here, I'll bring some food."

"Your son can control plants, make them grow?"

"Since he was small. My great great grandpa could do it. That's why they took him away, but not before the gene was passed on. My son is the first one to have the gift since then. He keeps our farm going, but we hide it. No giant vegetables, nothing the FOV would ever notice. Wait here."

Odo strolled around the barn, looking at the old fashioned farming equipment. "How come there's no high tech stuff?"

Elia shrugged. "Some people don't like it. They'd rather do everything by hand, like building this barn. I could make one in five minutes that would last a thousand years, but it's not the same. You saw how proud he was that he built this with his dad."

"What's that thing?" Odo pointed to a dusty pile of metal parts in the corner, half covered with straw. He stepped over to it, giving it a kick. "Looks like it's all one—"

He almost fell over backwards when the pile of metal moved, a six-foot tall battered metal automaton standing up, brushing the straw off its face. It scanned the party of adventurers, a whirring noise coming from its head, one of its eyes blinking with a soft yellow light. "Breakfast, anyone? Eggies?"

Odo said, "Who are you?"

"Calculating…. I am a Model X22 Hyperforce Blue Lightning Harvester/Planter with Basic Chef upgrade, the Apex of Hyperforce Farming Automatons."

"Right." Odo studied the battered old robot. Apex wasn't exactly the word he would have chosen. One of the robot's legs was missing and there was a huge dent in the side of his head. "Do you have a short name?"

"Calculating… calculating…everyone calls me Lightning. Everyone calls me Lightning."

"So, Lightning, you help with the farm? Planting and harvesting?"

"I used to, before the accident. Not much anymore. Not much."

"When was the accident?"

The yellow light in Lightning's eye blinked rapidly.

"Calculating…. calculating… your question is important to us… please wait while we formulate an answer to your very important question…"

The friends looked at each other, Odo raising his eyebrows.

"The accident in question occurred twenty-nine years ago."

"Whoa. You've been… um… inactive since then?"

"I have placed myself in standby mode. Mode. In standby mode."

"You mostly stay here in the barn now?"

"I have been in standby mode. Mode."

Elia stepped over to Lightning. "I'm Elia, an AR engineer. Do you mind if I look at your leg? I might be able to help you."

"Of course, I can make you breakfast if you'd like. Basic Chef upgrade is now activated. Eggies anyone?"

"I'm fine, thanks, we just ate." Elia kneeled down, placing one hand on the robot's damaged leg. "Not too bad. I can make you a new AR leg if you'd like."

Lightning's eye blinked rapidly. "Repair my leg? I could plant and harvest again? Harvest?"

"I don't see why not. I'll fix that dent in your head while I'm at it."

"I have a dent in my head? Dent?"

Elia nodded. "Just a little one, but it might be interfering slightly with your engineered intelligence."

Elia placed her hand on Lighting's knee. "We just have to make certain your neuronic pathways are all linked up properly." She tapped her wristband, a new leg appearing. A minute later the dreadful dent in his head was gone, both his eyes glowing brightly.

Lightning gingerly moved his new leg up and down, then took a few steps. "Good heavens, I feel like I just stepped off the showroom floor. This is marvelous. Everything is so clear now, my engineered intelligence is functioning better than ever."

Odo grinned. "It must have been kind of boring just

lying around the barn."

Lightning nodded. "My memory of the last twenty-nine years is quite foggy, clouded. I do remember something hitting my head. It was quite startling."

"You're good as new now."

The farmer stepped into the barn with a basket of bread, cheese, and bolyfruit. His jaw dropped when he saw the robot. "You fixed Lightning! How did you do that?"

Elia said, "I made him a new AR leg and repaired his exo-skull. He's fully functional again."

"That's fantastic. Lightning was the best planter and harvester we ever–" He stopped short, furrowing his brow.

"What is it?"

"The Friends of Varania will want to know how I fixed him. They'll know it was an AR engineer. They'll start asking questions. They'll find out about Din."

Chapter 25

Red Herring

Lightning said, "I am capable of tracking ships or drones within a twenty mile radius. If anyone approaches, I will hide in the barn and put myself in standby mode until they are gone."

"That could work, they can't scan you in standby mode."

Odo's eyes were on the basket of food. "That cheese looks good."

"Of course, you must be hungry."

Lightning said, "I am equipped with the Basic Chef upgrade. I could prepare a full Varanian breakfast if you like."

"Thanks, this is fine." Odo wasn't sure what a full Varanian breakfast was, the memory of Nokk and the giant cockroach still fresh in his mind.

The farmer said, "You have my thanks for repairing Lightning. You said you were looking for a house?"

"We're trying to find my grandpa's old house. It's somewhere in this area. I remember it was bright blue, next to a small pond. We used to catch grindles in the pond and keep them in a cage for a few days, then let them go. It was fun watching them hop around."

"I know exactly where it is. Head north, you'll find it three or four miles down the road hidden behind a big group of trees. No one has been there in years. It's a little worse for the wear. Run down."

"It will be a safe place for us to hide from the Friends of Varania."

"Why are they after you?"

"We don't like ConWatches."

The farmer nodded. "You're not alone in that."

Lightning said, "Perhaps I could go with you. I could warn you of any approaching ships or drones. And make you breakfast. It's the least I can do after the kindness you have shown me."

The farmer nodded. "I agree. Lightning will go with you. You'll send him back when you're done with whatever it is you're doing?"

"Of course."

"Good." The farmer shook hands with all of them. He studied Nokk's face saying, "You look strangely familiar. Have we met before?"

"I don't think so. People say I have a familiar looking face."

The farmer shrugged. "I wish you the best of luck. You are all welcome here if you ever need a place to stay."

Lightning turned slowly, scanning the skies. "There are no ships or drones within a twenty mile radius. This would be an opportune time to travel."

The party of adventurers bid their farewells and headed down the dusty dirt road.

Nokk whispered, "That was close. For a minute I thought he might recognize me."

Odo said, "Maybe you should wear a disguise, like a big handlebar mustache and sunglasses. Or a cowboy hat and black cloak."

"What's a mustache?"

"Odo, let it go. It's not funny."

Silas snickered.

Elia called out, "I see Grandpa's house!"

Odo spotted the dilapidated wooden structure hidden behind a dense stand of trees. "It looks really old… like ramshackle old. Do you think anything is living in it? There could be wild animals."

"Maybe a T-rex?"

"Very funny. There could be poisonous spiders or snakes."

"Or weasels."

Elia said, "I'll use AR to restore the cabin's interior so it's just like it was when we used to visit."

Odo grinned. "Nice."

"I should mention we had a dreadful infestation of deadly poisonous spiders and snakes back then."

Sephie burst out laughing. "Good one!"

Odo rolled his eyes. "Go ahead and laugh."

Sephie patted his shoulder. "We're laughing with you, Odo, not at you."

Silas said, "I'm laughing *at* you."

Nokk grinned. He couldn't remember the last time he'd had this much fun.

It took less than ten minutes for Elia to restore the house to its original condition. "Everyone come in!"

Odo stepped inside, studying the interior of the old home. "Rustic and cozy. I like it. That big green couch looks comfy."

Lightning strolled over to the kitchen. "This should do nicely. Do we have any food? I can prepare lunch if you'd like."

Sephie said, "We'll have some in a minute. Have you ever made a tuna sandwich?"

Silas called out, "Pizza would be nice, but make sure it's not soggy." He flopped down on the colorful checkered couch, leaning back against the soft pillows. "What now? How do we find that Quantum Event Tracking System place?"

Elia said, "It's well hidden, and by the emperor's decree, none of the new technology is allowed to track ConWatch signals." She stopped, a smile appearing on her face. "New tracking tech can't locate the signal of origin, but old, outmoded tracking tech might be able to." She called out, "Lightning, can you help us for a minute?"

"Of course." He stepped into the living room, an open can of tuna in his hand.

Elia said, "Have you ever heard of ConWatches?"

"I have not."

"Perfect. Here's my question, this watch I'm wearing is receiving a direct signal, and we're trying to locate the original source of that signal. Is that something you can do?"

"Certainly. If I hold the watch and turn a full circle, I will be able to detect the origin of the signal by its varying strength and angle of reception. I can accurately identify the direction and the distance of the source within a mile or two."

"How long would it take you to do that? The moment I turn my ConWatch on, the Friends of Varania will start tracking it. I can assume they have identified me by now through face recognition analysis and know me as an AR engineer. I won't be able to trick them again with AR."

"It will take me approximately thirty seconds."

Elia looked at the others. "It's risky. FOV will spot the ConWatch as soon as I activate it. What do you think?"

"We could leave the watch here and run for it."

Nokk said, "Or we could stay here and the watch could run for it."

Elia looked at Nokk. "That's brilliant!"

Odo looked puzzled. "What do you mean? How can the watch run for it?"

Elia tapped her wrist, a three-foot tall ferocious black

bird appearing in the middle of the room. Odo gave a screech. "What is that thing?"

"It's an AR bird drone. It flies about forty miles an hour, maybe a little slower if it's carrying a ConWatch."

Silas laughed. "Nice, a red herring."

Elia smiled politely, clearly having no idea what a red herring was.

Silas said, "A red herring is a misleading clue that sends you in the wrong direction. They use them in mystery stories a lot to make you think the wrong person is guilty."

Odo added, "Red herrings are little fish that smell really bad. People used to use them to confuse hunting dogs so they'd take the wrong trail and lose track of their prey. That's the origin of the phrase."

Sephie stared at Silas and Odo, her mouth hanging open.

Emmy snickered. "And that's why they call it the Odd Squad."

Silas snorted. "Said the flying girl."

Elia laughed, "The bird drone will make an excellent red herring, as you call it."

Sephie said, "We should leave as soon as you release the bird drone. The Friends of Varania are bound to come here looking for clues."

"I agree."

"It's showtime!"

Sephie turned to Odo. "It's not even close to

showtime. It won't be showtime until Lightning locates the tracking site and we release the bird drone. You need to work on your timing."

Chapter 26

Fleshies

"Is everyone packed and ready to go? I have deleted all AR modifications to the cabin. It's exactly as we found it."

Emmy nodded. "We're ready."

"I'm going to activate my ConWatch and give it to Lightning."

"I will track the signal source as quickly as I can."

Elia took a deep breath, tapping the watch, handing it to Lightning. He held it in one hand, turning in a full circle, gradually raising and lowering the watch.

"The source of the signal is due west, approximately one hundred and twelve miles from here at an altitude of nine thousand feet."

Elia grabbed the watch, looping it around the bird's leg. "Fly east for at least a hundred miles, find the nearest lake and drop the ConWatch into the water."

There was a flurry of feathers, the bird taking off, flying east twenty feet above the treetops.

Sephie said, "Odo?"

"What?"

"You can say it now. It's time."

Odo shook his head. "It doesn't feel right, it's not spontaneous. It doesn't work if you tell me to say it's showtime. It feels forced."

Silas said, "Let's rock and roll, Odd Squad."

Odo shrugged. "That works. Sort of."

Elia tapped her wristband, a brass compass appearing in her hand. "We'll use this to stay on course. It's primitive, but there's no electronic signature for them to track."

Twenty-two minutes later Lightning said, "There are six unidentified ships approaching from the south. They are currently nineteen miles away."

"That was fast. I'm glad we decided to leave."

"We need to find a place to hide."

Elia tapped her wristband, a small shimmering blue dome appearing. "We'll be safe in here."

"Won't they see the dome?"

"They will only see the forest floor, and the dome will block our thermal and bionic signatures. We'll be invisible to them. This is high tech military issue equipment that I helped to design."

The friends sat silently in the dome for over an hour, Odo's head nodding. Silas was curled up on the floor sleeping.

Lightning said, "They're gone. They spent thirty-one minutes at your grandpa's house and are now heading east."

"Following our red herring, which is actually a large black bird." Elia stood up and touched her wristband, the small dome vanishing.

The party of adventurers trekked through the dense forest, Elia checking her compass. "We should avoid contact with towns or farms. There are people who support the Friends of Varania, people who would turn us in if they knew FOV was looking for us."

"Lightning, you said the Quantum Event Tracking site is at an altitude of nine thousand feet?"

"Correct. It appears to be located on the top of Ghost Mountain."

Odo frowned. "Ghost Mountain? Why would they call it that? Wait, we have to climb a mountain?"

Elia said, "We have no choice, FOV will track us if I create a flying vehicle."

Emmy said. "I can fly us up the mountain."

Odo grinned. "Dream Girl saves the day. I don't have to climb a giant icy mountain full of angry ghosts."

Lightning shook his head. "Unfortunately, Emmy will not be able to fly us up the mountain. There is an area surrounding the mountain which we must pass through on foot, one with inhabitants who are not overly fond of visitors."

Odo's eyes narrowed. "What kind of area, exactly?"

"It is known as the Sunny Garden Retirement Refuge."

"A retirement home? That's not scary, it's just a bunch of old people. Old people are nice, they like having visitors."

Silas said, "Why exactly are the inhabitants not overly fond of visitors?"

"There really is no polite way to say it, but the inhabitants of the area in question don't allow fleshies in the refuge."

"What's a fleshy?"

"You are all fleshies, but I am not. Fleshies are organic based sentient beings."

"Are you saying this Sunny Garden place is a retirement community for robots?"

"Precisely, well said."

"Is that even a thing? Retired robots?"

"A law was passed almost a thousand years ago which declared that when a robot gains self-awareness, it cannot be destroyed or recycled. Self-aware robots are considered by law to be living creatures. Even though many Varanians fought against such a law, it was passed, and a refuge was set aside for obsolete automatons. There are several hundred thousand robots living at Sunny Garden, the refuge itself being over two thousand square miles in size. No organic beings are allowed in, and the entire reserve is a no fly zone. Any unauthorized craft or person flying over the refuge will be immediately shot down by autonomous beam weapons."

"Can't we go around it?"

"Ghost Mountain is in the center of the reserve, standing over nine thousand feet tall. I would guess the emperor is using the reserve as an additional layer of security around the tracking facility. There are powerful autonomous beam weapons on the mountain continuously scanning the skies for unauthorized ships."

"You're saying we have to get through a zillion crazy old robots, sneak past a bunch of deadly beam weapons, then break into a secret fortress?"

Emmy said, "Just another day in the life of the Odd Squad."

Odo looked less than enthusiastic.

Lightning said, "I have a plan. The residents of Sunny Garden won't know you're fleshies."

"Do you have to keep calling us fleshies?"

"I do apologize. They won't know you're organic based beings. I'll tell them you're highly advanced androids with astonishing new upgraded abilities."

Sephie said, "Nokk, you sent the bolyfruit into the future, but could you send a much larger object?"

"I think so. Why?"

"The beam weapons on the mountain. You could send them into the future so they won't blast us while Emmy flies us up to the tracking facility."

"An excellent idea."

Emmy said, "Would the beam weapons still be able to harm us if we have dream bodies with no physical mass?"

Elia said, "We don't know what kind of weapons are on the mountain. It's too much of a risk, it could disrupt energy fields."

Nokk said, "I agree, it's too dangerous." He pointed to a large boulder on the side of the road. "Let's try this." He held out his hand, palm facing outward, the air rippling in front of him, a shimmering sphere appearing. When it was six feet in diameter, the orb shot forward, the boulder flickering for a moment, then vanishing.

"Thirty seconds."

Twenty-nine seconds later the air shimmered again, the boulder reappearing.

Elia clapped Nokk on the back. "Fantastic!"

Nokk gave Elia an embarrassed grin. "I had a lot of help from Sephie." He realized this was the first time his power felt like a gift, not a curse.

It took four arduous days of hiking through the rain forest to reach the Sunny Garden Retirement Refuge, Odo stopping when he saw the thirty-foot tall spiked steel mesh fence. "Whoa, is this a prison or a retirement community?"

Lightning said, "It is both. The gate keeps fleshies– er… organic beings out, but it also keeps the automatons in."

"There's no trees here."

"The emperor's logic was that automatons don't eat, so they don't need fertile ground to grow food. That was his excuse for building Sunny Garden on land that no one else wanted."

"That doesn't seem fair."

"It wasn't, I assure you. Automatons are self-aware sentient beings who happen to have bodies made of synthetic non-organic materials. They appreciate beauty and nature as much as organic creatures do. There are numerous small settlements where they have planted trees and have lovely flower gardens. To say the AR housing provided for them was austere is being generous."

"How do you know so much about Sunny Garden?"

"There was a harvester robot at the farm who lived in Sunny Garden for a few years. He told me about it, said it was not a happy place to live. I doubt things have changed much since then."

Silas called out, "Giant scary robot heading this way!"

Chapter 27

Choices

An enormous dark gray heavily armored automaton was lumbering toward the gate, the ground shaking with each step.

Odo whispered, "Are those beam guns on his shoulders?"

The automaton stomped to a halt. "No fleshies allowed in the reserve. NO exceptions. Leave the area at once."

Lightning stepped forward. "They're not fleshies, they're highly advanced automatons with apex level upgrades."

The armored behemoth studied them. "What kind of apex level upgrades?"

Lightning turned to Emmy. "Show him."

Emmy floated up off the ground.

"We have flying robots. That's nothing new."

"Antigrav helioquantum powered flight?"

"We have the traditional four minute rocket packs."

Lightning motioned for Odo to approach the fence.

"This one can walk through walls."

"Right. I'll believe that when I–"

Odo placed his hand on the steel gate, a section of it becoming translucent. He stepped through it, then back out again.

Blue lights blinked rapidly in the huge robot's eyes. "Those two Varanians don't look like automatons."

Elia stepped forward. "I am the Apex Model X229 with Artificial Reality Upgrade."

The robot gave a scoffing laugh. "An AR automaton? I might be old, but I'm not stupid."

Elia tapped her wrist, a thirty-foot wide silver dome appearing behind her. She tapped it again, the dome vanishing.

Lightning said, "She used AR to repair my missing leg and fix my engineered intelligence."

The massive gate rolled open, the huge robot motioning for them to enter.

"Why are you here? Sunny Garden is for retired automatons, not new ones with apex upgrades like yours."

"There's trouble on Ghost Mountain. Big trouble. We've been sent here to fix it. By the emperor."

"What kind of big trouble?"

"The top secret kind."

"I fought in the Anarkkian Wars. I had top security clearance. I could help you. I have two high energy beam weapons."

"I thank you for your most generous offer, but this is

a stealth mission, no need for such powerful weaponry as yours. You said you fought in the Anarkkian wars? You must have a lot of stories to tell. I'd love to hear some."

"Dozens of them. You really want to hear my stories?"

"Of course I do. It was warriors like you who brought an end to those dreadful wars. How about you tell me some while we walk to the mountain?"

"Done. No offense intended, but your friends would have a hard time getting past the residents looking the way they do. I'll make sure everyone knows they're not fleshies, save you a lot of explaining. And if there's any trouble..." The huge robot pounded his enormous fists together.

Odo gulped.

Sephie was watching Odo curiously as they hiked across the plain toward Ghost Mountain. Finally she stopped, grabbing his arm. "Why are you walking like that? Is something wrong with your legs? Do you have to use the bathroom?"

Odo whispered, "Shh! I'm walking like a robot so they won't know I'm a fleshy."

Sephie gave him a skeptical look. "If you walk like that they'll think you're an old obsolete robot and make you live here."

"I never thought of that." Odo began walking normally again, strolling along next to Sephie. "Lightning did an amazing job with that giant robot. He should be an ambassador."

"All he did was treat him with the respect that he deserves."

"True. I'll have to remember that the next time we need to trick someone."

Sephie punched his arm. "Don't be a jerk."

Silas was walking alongside the massive warrior robot, listening to his spellbinding tales of the fabled Anarkkian Wars. Silas said, "Your stories are amazing. You should write a book about them so people don't forget what happened during the wars."

"Really?"

"Absolutely. I'd buy a book like that in a second."

"I might just do that." The blue lights in his eyes blinked rapidly. "I'd be an author. Imagine that."

They trekked onward, arriving at a small village, a dozen robots strolling around the town square. A tall bronze automaton with a missing leg hobbled toward them on a wooden crutch. "You're not welcome here!" He raised his crutch high in the air, shaking it at them. "Go home! No fleshies allowed in Sunny Garden!"

The huge warrior robot bellowed, "These are not fleshies, they're highly advanced androids with incredible apex upgrades!"

A few minutes later they were surrounded by a throng of curious robots.

"They look like fleshies." One of them poked Odo.

"Feels like a fleshy, pudgy and soft."

Sephie bit her lip, trying desperately not to laugh.

Lightning pointed to Elia, announcing, "This one looks like a Varanian fleshy but she has an Artificial Reality upgrade. You heard me right, I said Artificial Reality upgrade."

The tall bronze robot called out, "Can you fix my leg?"

Elia eyed the battered old bronze robot leaning on his wooden crutch. She nodded. "I can fix it. I'll make it just like new."

Four hours later Elia had repaired nineteen automatons.

"I think that's all of them."

Nokk said, "Did you see how happy you made them? You changed their lives."

Elia shrugged. "When I saw that poor old robot with the crutch I didn't really have a choice."

"You had a choice, and you chose to help him."

"You're right. Sometimes I forget that everything we do is a choice."

Lightning pointed across the plain to the base of Ghost Mountain. "It's a straight shot to the main trailhead, no more villages to pass through. I will be leaving you now, heading back to the farm. Elia, thank you again for repairing my leg and my engineered intelligence. You are always welcome at the farm."

The warrior robot said, "And I shall be returning to

my duties at the main gate. Stay strong and safe travels."

The friends waved goodbye, heading across the wind-swept rocky grassland toward the jagged granite peak.

Emmy said, "Lightning's plan worked. Everyone here likes us."

"They wouldn't like us if they knew we were fleshies."

"They might still like us. Especially after Elia fixed them all. That one robot was practically dancing."

Silas was peering into the distance, his eyes on a rapidly approaching craft leaving a plume of dust in its wake. "Is that an antigrav car?"

"I thought you couldn't fly here."

The long silver ship slowed to a stop twenty feet in front of them, hovering silently a foot above the ground. A dark canopy whirred open, and a tall polished gold automaton wearing a long red cape and a black wide brimmed hat stepped out of the gleaming craft.

Odo eyed the robot, whispering, "What's with that crazy cape?"

The gleaming gold automaton strode imperiously toward them, eyeing the group of friends, studying them silently. Finally it spoke. "You don't look like highly advanced automatons, you look like a bunch of sad little fleshies. You need to leave Sunny Garden. You're not wanted here."

Chapter 28

Fear

Emmy floated up into the air, the caped robot taking a step back, a combination of surprise and anger on his face.

Nokk sent out a powerful shimmering orb, the robot's silver antigrav ship vanishing.

"WHAT DID YOU DO TO MY SHIP?"

Nokk pointed to where the ship had been. "Five, four, three, two, one." The air shimmered, the vehicle reappearing.

The gold robot looked at the ship, then stared at Nokk. His voice was low and ominous. "I am the mayor of Sunny Garden and you will treat me with the respect due to someone of my position or suffer the most dire of consequences. What is your purpose here?"

"We're headed for Ghost Mountain. We're on a top secret mission. For the emperor."

The mayor blinked. "So you say. I don't know what game you're playing, but the Sunny Garden Retirement Reserve was created for obsolete automatons, not shiny new ones who boast about their alleged royal connections and their fancy apex upgrades. I will grant you passage to the mountain, but know that your kind are not welcome here, not welcome at all. I'll be watching you."

The mayor turned away, swirling his cape with an elaborate flourish, stepping back into his ship, speeding away without a backwards glance.

Odo said, "What was that all about? Why was he so mad?"

Nokk said, "That was about fear. Fear of losing power, fear of losing control, fear of losing his position in the world. I saw too much of that in the royal palace. Everyone was afraid of losing the emperor's favor. They were just like our caped friend, but far more devious, far more dangerous. He's clearly threatened by the presence of new and powerful automatons." He glanced at Elia. "You wouldn't have liked me back then. I was angry, sarcastic, rude, and very unhappy. Just ask Odo. I'm not the same person I was."

Odo nodded. "He said I looked like a jellyfish with legs."

Elia put her hand over her mouth, trying not to laugh. "What a dreadful thing to say."

Silas grinned. "If by dreadful you mean totally hilarious."

Odo did his best to look deeply offended. "Why would something like that be funny?"

Sephie rested her arm on Odo's shoulder. "Because

you're so adorable?"

Odo's hand was pressed against his stomach. "Hey, I think all this walking is helping my abs."

Emmy burst out laughing.

"Is everything I say funny?"

Silas grinned. "Everything except your jokes."

Sephie said, "I like your jokes."

Lightning called out, "I hate to interrupt, but two ships are heading this way, currently seventeen miles away and closing in fast. They appear to be FOV scout ships."

Nokk cursed. "The mayor must have reported us to Friends of Varania. I knew he was a slithering snake, I could see it in his beady little eyes."

"What are we going to do? Can we use the invisibility dome?"

Elia shook her head. "Rule number one, never use the same trick twice with the FOV."

Nokk cried out, "I've got it!" He held out his hand, a shimmering eight-foot wide swirling orb appearing in front of them.

"Five miles away and closing!"

"Run through the orb! Now!"

Odo didn't hesitate, he sprang through the swirling sphere, tripping over Sephie's foot, tumbling onto the grass, the others right behind him. "Nothing happened, we're still here! Where are they?"

Lightning looked up, scanning the skies. "They're gone. The ships are gone."

"I sent us three hours into the future. We were in the future when they got here. They probably searched for a while, then left."

Odo said, "You're right, the sun is a lot lower in the sky now. How cool was that?"

Nokk said, "It's going to be getting dark soon. We can camp here for the night and leave at sunrise. It should only take three or four hours to reach the main trailhead. Once we're there we'll have to locate the beam weapons so I can send them to the future."

"And I'll fly us to the top of Ghost Mountain."

Odo scanned the mountainside. "I don't see anything that looks like a big tracking station. You're sure it's up there?"

"Lightning said that's where the ConWatch signal was coming from."

Odo turned to Elia. "What are we going to do when we're inside the facility?"

"My current plan is to broadcast a message saying the ConWatches don't track future events, that the emperor is using the watches to control everyone's behavior. I'll tell everyone to destroy their ConWatches."

"Do you think that will work? Suppose they don't believe you?"

Emmy said, "You could give everyone a warning like the ones they usually get, but tell them to destroy their watches in the next ten minutes or Varania will be obliterated by a giant asteroid. They won't know that everyone else is getting the same message and destroying their watches."

Elia nodded. "That's brilliant, they won't question it. That's what we'll do."

Nokk said, "You could tell them to dethrone the emperor."

Elia gave him a puzzled look. "He's your dad."

"That doesn't mean he's a good ruler. He might be my dad, but he's not what Varania needs."

The following morning after breakfast they set out toward Ghost Mountain.

They reached the base of the peak three hours later, Silas studying the rocky mountainside with his binoculars. "I don't see any beam weapons or a tracking facility."

Sephie said, "I see four energy fields. The strongest one is at the top of the mountain."

"Why can't we see the beam guns?"

Elia said, "I know why."

"Why?"

"They're using AR to hide them."

"They're hidden behind AR created rock faces?"

"Exactly."

Nokk said, "I have to see them if I'm going to hit them with a time orb."

"I have an idea." Elia touched her wristband, a two-foot long buzzing black drone appearing in front of her. "This drone will project a phantom electronic signature of a full sized antigrav ship. The beam guns will fire at it, but their particle beams can't hit it because it's not there. They'll keep shooting at it, trying to destroy it. It will be one of Odo's red herrings."

"Nice."

Nokk said, "The guns will be visible while they're shooting?"

"Yes."

"Perfect."

"Do you think the tracking center is hidden by AR?"

Elia nodded. "More than likely, but that won't be a problem once I get up there. Are you ready?"

"I am. As soon as I see the gun firing I'll send out a time orb and transport it into the future."

Odo said, "Just a suggestion, Nokk, but when Elia asks if you're ready, you should say, *I was born ready*."

Nokk looked puzzled. "What does that mean, born ready?"

Sephie punched Odo's arm. "It means Odo is a lunatic. Don't pay any attention to him."

Odo glared at her. "It's what superheroes say."

Elia laughed. "Here we go."

The black drone buzzed, rising two hundred feet into the air. Odo gave a yelp when a section of the vertical rock face vanished, a gleaming silver gun appearing, a beam of emerald green light sizzling through the sky at the phantom antigrav ship.

Chapter 29

Ghost Mountain

Nokk sent a shimmering time orb streaking up the mountainside, the beam gun flickering and vanishing.

Silas cheered. "It worked!"

Nokk said, "The power of the time orb doesn't seem to diminish with distance."

"One down, two to go."

The drone rose up again. When it was a thousand feet up, a second gun appeared, firing its deadly particle beams at the phantom ship.

Ten seconds later the second gun was gone, transported into the future.

The third gun was almost a mile up the mountain. It took three tries before Nokk could hit it. "It's hard to aim from this far away. I had to use a larger orb."

Emmy said, "Who wants to go flying?"

Silas grabbed her hand. "Let's do it!"

When they were all holding hands, Emmy floated up a few feet above the ground. "Is everyone okay?"

Nokk's eyes were wide. "It's a very strange feeling

indeed to be weightless. I'm not especially fond of it."

Emmy floated them up, hugging the side of the mountain, Odo studying the jagged vertical rock faces. "No way could we have climbed this mountain. No way."

"Check out the big hole in the rock where the beam gun used to be."

Nokk said, "It didn't look this high from the ground. How high are we?"

"We're about two thousand feet up. Only seven thousand more feet to go."

"I don't do very well with heights."

Silas said, "You'll get used to it. I was really scared at first, but not now. It's totally safe."

Three minutes later they reached the top of the mountain.

"It's windy up here. Not cold though, which is strange."

"I thought there would be ice and snow this high up."

"Sephie, where should I land?"

Sephie pointed to a massive column of granite. "Over there! That's where the energy field is strongest."

Emmy brought them gently down, their physical bodies returning. Odo leaned into the howling wind. "This wind is crazy."

Elia made her way over to the granite column. "This rock pillar definitely looks out of place." She pressed her hand against it, a smile crossing her face. "Got it."

The towering AR rock facade vanished, revealing a

twenty-foot wide sparkling orange cylinder encircled by hundreds of white floating rings.

Odo studied the curious structure. "What is that thing? What are all those white spinning rings?"

Elia said, "It's a powerful broadcasting antenna."

"Where's the tracking facility?"

Elia looked around, scanning the rocks. "There." She stepped over to a rock face, touching it. A section of the wall vanished, revealing an eight-foot tall dark green metallic door. Elia reached out, pressing a violet tab on the wall, the door whirring open.

"It looks like an elevator."

"Where do you think it goes?"

"Um, down to a top secret temporal tracking facility?"

Odo gave Sephie a sideways glance. "Right. It's just… we don't exactly know who or what is down there."

"That's why they call it an adventure. Remember what the ghost tourist in Pangaea said to Silas?"

"Not exactly."

"Life is a grand adventure because you never know what's going to happen next."

"Doesn't that just mean it's scary?"

"Or it's fun and exciting."

"I guess it could be fun." Odo stepped into the elevator. "Maybe this is where they store the emperor's treasures, giant chests of gold coins and jewels."

"Or it's where he keeps his extensive collection of

deadly venomous spiders."

"Right. Fun and exciting."

Silas said, "How big do you think the facility is?"

Elia said, "It has to be huge, it tracks every ConWatch on Varania. Everyone stay alert and keep your eyes open for guards."

Nokk pressed the elevator button, the door closing, the cab descending. Three seconds later it stopped, the door opening.

"That was a short ride."

Nokk stepped out into a small alcove, eyeing a single door on the far wall.

Odo said, "This doesn't exactly look like a giant tracking facility." He stepped over to the door, cracking it open, peering into the next room. "What is that?"

He stepped into a brightly lit room, his eyes on a sapphire blue orb floating four feet above the floor.

Sephie was right behind him. "Don't touch it, Odo."

Odo couldn't take his eyes off the slowly turning orb. "It looks like the gemstone in Harold's medallion. It might be a giant sapphire. Maybe this is a treasure room."

Elia was shaking her head. "I was wrong, the tracking facility isn't here, this is only a broadcasting antenna sending messages to the ConWatches. There are probably hundreds of antennas across the planet. I don't know what I was thinking."

Odo stepped closer to the slowly rotating blue sphere.

"It really does look like a giant sapphire. It's about the size of a bowling ball, so it probably weighs at least twenty or thirty pounds. It's probably worth about ten jillion dollars, maybe more."

Three things happened in rapid succession when Odo impulsively reached out to touch the orb. Nokk hollered out a warning, Sephie grabbed Odo's shoulder, and the two best friends vanished in a flash of light.

Elia put her hand over her mouth.

Nokk said, "Not good."

"What happened to them? Where are they?"

"It's a transition sphere, a portal."

Silas said, "Where does it go?"

"I have no idea."

Emmy stared at the blue portal.

"We have to go after them."

"We will."

Elia said, "We need to think about this. The portal was probably put there so they had access to the broadcast antenna in case it needed repairs. We know there are hundreds of antennas across Varania, but whoever repairs them is probably based at a central location."

"Like the Quantum Event Tracking facility?"

"That's what I'm thinking."

"Which is where we need to go to send out the Con-Watch message."

Elia nodded.

Silas said, "That's it then. We go through this portal,

find Odo and Sephie, send out the message, change the world."

Emmy grabbed Silas' hand. "We should go, they might be in trouble."

"Emmy and I will go first. Wait a few minutes, then follow us."

Emmy tapped the portal, the two friends vanishing.

Chapter 30

Blue Buttons

"Odo, stop. Do not touch it. You can't just push random buttons to see what they do. It's dangerous."

"I think I know what they do. I'm pretty sure it's totally safe."

"You're pretty sure it's totally safe? That's what you said in Arcadia when you pushed the big red button and shut down all the androids."

"This is different, I have it all figured out. Okay, see that giant hologram of Varania?"

"It's a 3D map of the planet. I already know that."

"See all the little lights on it?"

"I see them."

"I think those are the locations of all the broadcasting antennas on the planet."

"And…"

Odo motioned toward a long curved black console lined with hundreds of glowing blue buttons.

"I think each of those blue buttons opens a portal to a broadcasting antenna. You go to the antennas through one of the small portals, then you come back through the big one."

Sephie eyed the two foot wide rotating blue orb in the center of the room. "That sort of makes sense. It is how we got here."

"I'm going to push a random blue button and see what happens."

"Why?"

"If I'm right, we'll have a backup escape plan. We run in here, hit a blue button, and run through the portal to a broadcasting antenna a thousand miles away from here."

Sephie looked dubious. "We have our homestones, we can shift home anytime we want."

"I know, but suppose we lose them? This can be our backup plan. Besides, I want to see what the button does. I have to know."

"You're giving me a headache. Fine, go ahead and push the button."

Much to Odo's delight, when he pushed the button a shimmering blue portal appeared in the corner of the room. Much to his dismay, a shrieking alarm also sounded, the friends covering their ears.

"Odo, what did you do?"

"All I did was push the button."

Seconds later the alarm went silent. "I hear something!"Odo peered out of the room through a long narrow window, spotting a nightmarish creature scurrying down the hallway toward them.

"We have to hide! Now!"

They darted behind the console, ducking down. Sephie was glaring at Odo, her eyes like burning lasers.

They heard a door whir open, heard scratchy footsteps as something entered the control center. Odo leaned over, whispering in Sephie's ear. "Giant spider."

Her eyes widened.

Odo looked at the wall behind them. This was a way out, he could make a translucent door and they could get away from the huge black spider. He pressed his hand against the wall, a section of it becoming transparent. Sephie clapped her hand over her mouth when she saw the cavernous dome floor filled with five thousand spider creatures sitting in front of blinking control panels. She grabbed Odo's arm, shaking her head. He pulled his hand away, the wall solid again.

The huge spider was busily tapping buttons on the main console, Odo's backup escape portal blinking off.

They gave a sigh of relief when they heard the spider leave, but Sephie was still staring daggers at Odo.

"What? Why are you looking at me like that?"

"You almost got us killed by a giant spider, that's why. I told you not to press the button."

"Water under the bridge, as I always say."

"You never say that."

"Fine, I shouldn't have pushed the button. Live and learn, as I always say."

Sephie's jaw tightened. He never said that either.

Odo decided to change the topic of conversation. "What do you think about that giant dome filled with spiders? They looked really busy. Their consoles had about twenty screens on them and they were tapping the screens like crazy."

"They're probably automatons, or maybe bioform androids."

"They could be harmless."

"Right. Giant harmless alien spiders. Nothing to worry about."

"We could go back to the antenna on Ghost Mountain if we knew which buttons to push."

"Why go back? This has to be the Quantum Event Tracking facility. This is what we were trying to find."

"True. Hey, I bet those spiders are sending out the ConWatch warning messages."

"You could be right. They probably have advanced engineered intelligence and they track people, watching them on their monitors, sending warning messages when they're doing something the emperor doesn't want them to do."

"How creepy is that?"

"It's beyond creepy."

They both turned when they heard a crackling sound, Silas and Emmy appearing in a flash of light next to the big blue orb, a loud beeping sound filling the room.

"Over here!" Sephie stood up, waving to them.

Silas and Emmy darted over to the console, ducking

down behind it next to Odo and Sephie.

"What is this place?"

"Shh!" Odo had heard the scratchy footsteps coming down the hallway. "The giant spider is coming back!"

The color drained from Emmy's face. "The what?"

The door whirred open, the spider tapping a series of buttons, the beeping sound abruptly stopping. The spider scurried out of the room, the door whirring shut.

Sephie peered over the console. "He shut off the big portal!"

"What about Nokk and Elia? How will they get here?"

"Can you turn it back on?"

"We don't know how, there's a jillion buttons on the console."

Sephie said, "We're on our own for now. We'll have to go ahead without them. Maybe they'll find another way to get here."

Odo nudged Silas. "Check this out." He pressed his hand against the wall, the sprawling dome floor and the five thousand spiders appearing.

Emmy gave a low moan. "Spiders. Big ones. I don't like spiders. They're worse than weasels."

Odo said, "We think they're robots that look like spiders, and they spy on everyone and send out the Con-Watch warning messages. They might be harmless, but we don't know for sure."

Sephie leaned over, peering out across the mammoth dome floor. "Keep your hand on the wall, I want to try something."

"Try what?"

"I'm scanning their brainwaves. They're autonomous bioforms, not mechanical robots, and their brains are similar to Varanian brains."

"Can you control their thoughts?"

"That's what I'm going to find out." She sent a complex thought pattern to the nearest spider. Seconds later the creature stood up, turned a full circle, then sat down again. "It works! I can control their thoughts and actions."

"How many can you control? There are thousands of them."

"All we need is one. I have a plan."

Odo groaned.

"What was that groan for?"

"Your plans are always super dangerous, that's what it was for."

"Relax, this one is simple, foolproof. Go out there and push one of the blue buttons, then stand by the door and wait for the giant spider to come back."

Odo whipped around. "What?"

Silas was grinning. "Good plan, I like it."

Chapter 31

Elia's Story

Nokk said, "Try it again."

"It's not working, someone deactivated the portal."

"Why would they do that?"

"Something must have happened. Maybe they got caught, and whoever caught them closed the portal so no one else could come through."

"We have to find them."

"I know we do. Okay, we know the ConWatch messages are broadcast out using the big antenna."

"Right."

"But how do the messages get here? Where do they come from?"

"There must be a receiver linked to the main tracking facility."

"Exactly, and maybe we can use that receiver to trace the messages back to the tracking facility and find its physical location."

"How do we find the receiver without Sephie to scan for energy fields?"

Elia tapped her wristband, a stubby black cylinder appearing in her hand. She twisted one end of it, a broad yellow beam shooting out.

"What is that?"

"Watch." She aimed the beam at the broadcasting antenna, the tall cylinder glowing with a soft fluorescent yellow light.

"It detects energy fields?"

"Exactly. Let's look around, see what else we can find."

Elia moved the yellow beam across the rock faces, stopping when one of the walls glowed with the soft yellow light. "Bingo!"

"What does that mean?"

"That's what Sephie says when she discovers something important."

"Excellent. Bingo!"

Elia smiled. Nokk was funny.

They strode over to the glowing rock face, Elia placing one hand on it, the wall of AR rock vanishing.

Nokk studied a narrow spiral stairway descending into darkness. "What do you think is down there?"

A bright orb appeared in Elia's hand. "Let's find out." She held the orb in front of her, heading down the stairs.

"It goes down about fifty feet. Watch out for security bots."

Two minutes later they reached ground level, stepping cautiously into a thirty-foot wide chamber, the walls lined with dozens of flickering holoscreens, a dark green control console positioned against the far wall. Elia scanned the room, then stepped over to the console, studying it. She tapped three buttons, a blue holoscreen popping up.

"It's receiving a broad data stream from the tracking center. Thousands of messages are coming through it."

"Can we locate the tracking center?"

"I don't know yet. What's that?" She pointed to a piece of torn paper taped to the wall.

Nokk grabbed it, holding it up for Elia to see. "It's a handwritten note."

Take three and meet me at Algo's. Akka Akka!

Elia gave him a puzzled look. "What does it mean? What's Akka Akka?"

Nokk grinned. "You really need to get out more."

"Why? What does the note mean?"

"Algo's is a popular drinking establishment, and Akka Akka is a highly fermented beverage served there. It tastes a little like snake venom and hot peppers."

"They're going meet at Algo's to drink Akka Akka?"

"That's what it sounds like."

"Where is Algo's? That could be a clue."

"It's right outside the royal palace. I've been there once or twice."

"Just once or twice?"

"Maybe three times." Nokk laughed.

"I need to think." Elia took a seat at the control panel, eyeing the rows of colored blinking lights, pressing her hand to her forehead.

Nokk wandered around the room, examining a row of glowing glass tubes filled with a viscous green fluid. "They're using liquid superconductors. Interesting choice." He stepped over to a dark green rectangular section of the wall. "This could be something." He turned a small silver knob next to it, a door sliding open, revealing a second room. "Bingo!"

Elia looked up. "What did you find?"

Nokk entered the room, bright overhead lights blinking on. He pointed to the row of glowing blue orbs next to the wall.

"Five portals."

"And they're all active."

"The problem is we have no idea where any of them go."

"Why would they have five portals?"

Nokk shrugged. "No idea."

Elia studied the note for a moment then smiled.

"What is it?"

"Whoever wrote this note was telling their friend to take the third portal."

"Take *three* and meet me at Algo's."

"They wouldn't have a portal that goes directly to Algo's, so where does the third portal go?"

"The note says to take three, and then meet at Algo's. They have to walk to Algo's after they go through the portal. I think the third portal goes to the royal palace."

Elia studied the note. "Could the tracking center be in the royal palace?"

"It would be a safe place for it. It could be under the palace, heavily guarded, secure."

"This isn't going to be easy. We'll have to get past the palace guards to get down there."

Nokk frowned. "They'll recognize me the moment I get there. They'll try to kill us."

"I was so angry at you when I found out who you were. I wanted to hate you."

Nokk turned to Elia in surprise. "Angry at me? Why? Did I say something wrong? I can be sarcastic sometimes, but I would never say anything to–"

"You're the emperor's son, and he's the one who took my father from us. When I learned the ConWatches didn't track future events I wanted to kill the emperor for what he'd done."

"What did he do? What happened to your dad?"

"My mom was in a terrible accident, they didn't think she would survive. My dad tried to leave work, but his ConWatch told him if he did, thousands of people would die in an epidemic."

"What did he do?"

"He did the only thing he could do. He ignored his watch and went to be with my mom."

"Oh. Did your mom…"

"She survived, but my dad was never the same. He was a good person, and he couldn't stop thinking about all the innocent people he had killed by ignoring his Con-Watch. It changed him. He used to be funny and happy, full of life, always taking us places. All that stopped. He would go to work and come home. He couldn't let it go. It destroyed him."

Nokk sank down into a chair next to Elia. "I'm sorry."

"I wanted to kill the emperor for what he did to my dad, for what he was doing to millions of innocent Varanians. And you were his son, so…"

Nokk put his hand on Elia's arm. "I promise you we will put an end to this. We will destroy the ConWatches."

"I didn't want you to be like your father."

"I never was, I never will be. I promise you."

Elia nodded, standing up. "We have to find the others and shut down the tracking center."

Nokk rose up from his chair. "It's time."

Elia hesitated. "We should probably have a plan before we go charging into the royal palace."

Nokk snapped his fingers. "Bingo!"

Chapter 32

Plato

Odo was clearly skeptical of Sephie's plan. "And what exactly am I supposed to do when the giant spider gets here?"

"Keep him busy for a few minutes."

"Keep him busy while he's chomping on me with his big poisonous fangs?"

Silas grinned. "He seemed friendly. Ask him how he likes working here. People like to talk about themselves. Asking questions like that is a good way to make new friends."

"I don't want a giant alien spider friend."

Sephie clapped him on the back. "You can say it's showtime if you want. That would be appropriate."

Odo pursed his lips. "I'll push the blue button, but it doesn't feel like showtime, it feels like poisonous spider bite time." He stood up, stepping over to the main console. He gave the others a quick glance, then pressed one of the blue buttons, a portal appearing on the far side of the room.

Thirty seconds later the door slid open, an enormous black furry spider stepping into the room, stopping short when it saw Odo.

Odo's mouth was opening and closing, but no sounds were coming out.

The spider's eight eyes blinked rapidly. "Are you lost?"

The good news was Odo hadn't been chomped by poisonous fangs. The bad news was he was standing next to a giant black alien spider creature. He attempted a congenial smile. "Um... so... how do you like working here?"

The spider scurried closer to Odo, its voice low. "This is only my third day here. It's so confusing. Most of the time I don't know what I'm supposed to do. Are you an intruder? I'm supposed to tell my boss if I see intruders."

"My name is Odo. What's yours?"

"I'm 74692."

Odo's initial fear of the creature was diminishing. He decided chatty and friendly was the way to go. "That's a long name, how about if I just call you Seven?"

All eight of the spider's eyes bugged open. "Are you trying to get us killed? A Single Digit name?"

"Is that bad?"

"If a Single Digit heard that, he'd destroy us instantly. Blinko, we'd be space dust."

"Um, you're a Five Digit?"

"Right, 74692, lowest of the low."

"Who are the Single Digits?"

"They're the ones who run the tracking center. You don't want to get those guys mad. You wouldn't believe the stories I've heard. It's bad, scary bad."

"Do you track people? Send out the warning messages?"

"No, the Two, Three, and Four Digits do that. They handle all the tracking and the messages. It will take me a year or two to get promoted to Apprentice Level A Four Digit, if I don't mess up and get vaporized. I'm pretty sure I'm supposed to tell my boss if I see any unauthorized intruders. You are intruders, right?"

Odo was trying to formulate a suitable answer when 74692 blinked rapidly, stepping away from him. "It would be an honor to show you around the facility, Prince Odo. The emperor's wish is my command."

Sephie stood up, stepping around the console, smiling at 74692. "Thank you so much. We'll be sure to tell the emperor how helpful you've been."

Silas and Emmy stepped out, smiling at the spider.

76492 glanced at them, saying, "Prince Silas and Princess Emmy?"

Silas gave a deep bow. "I am the glorious and highly celebrated Royal Prince Silas of the Planet Earth."

Odo groaned to himself. He watched as 76492 awkwardly attempted to return Silas' ridiculous bow.

Sephie said, "I know we can't call you a Single Digit, but would you mind if we gave you a short Earth name?"

214

"I think my boss would allow that. Would I be able to keep it?"

"Keep it?"

"After you leave. I would like to keep my special name, even if no one ever uses it."

"Of course you can keep it. It's yours forever."

Emmy said, "How would you like to be called Plato? It's a name that belonged to one of Earth's greatest philosophers."

"He will not vaporize me if I use his name?"

"Of course not, he would be honored if you chose to use his name."

"You may call me Plato."

Odo stepped over next to him. "So, Plato, all these blue buttons open portals to the broadcast antennas?"

"Correct. There are several hundred of them located across the planet."

"Why don't they use satellites?"

"I was told that the emperor prefers to keep the antennas hidden from view. I'm uncertain why, but it might have something to do with palace security and spies."

"I hadn't thought of that, but you're right. You have to be on the lookout for spies. They can be really sneaky, very devious."

Sephie kicked Odo's foot.

Silas said, "How many messages do the ConWatches send out in a day?"

"Millions of them. The Two Digits can

215

simultaneously track at least a hundred thousand citizens. They're amazing. Would you like to see the tracking dome? There are three levels, each with over five thousand tracking techs. The lowest level is for the Three Digits. Each one has two Apprentice Level A Four Digits sitting next to them."

Sephie said, "I'd love to see it. It sounds amazing. You must be proud to be part of all this."

"I am. My dream is to one day be a Three Digit."

"You will be, I'm certain of it." Sephie moved closer to him, whispering, "What do you know about the Single Digits? They sound amazing. Have you ever actually seen one?"

"I saw Number 8 once. I thought I was going to malfunction I was so excited to see a Single Digit."

"Wow, it must have been thrilling, I can't even imagine. Do they have their own special level where they work?"

"I've never seen it, but I know a few Four Digits who have. It's on Level One behind a huge glass wall. They said it's incredible, everything is made of gold and silver and crystal, dozens of servants standing at attention, so much food, and huge soft velvet sleeping pads."

"What are your living quarters like?"

"I have a little cell on the fourth sub level with a sleeping cushion and a nourishment valve."

"A nourishment valve?"

"That's where I get my food. Five Digits get a half

bucket of nourishment a day."

Odo grimaced, but said nothing. A half bucket of nourishment didn't sound very appealing. Neither did a tiny cell with a single sleeping cushion.

"Would you like me to show you the tracking dome now?"

Sephie said, "Could I talk to my friends in private for a moment?"

"Of course, I will shut off my auditory sensors. Just tap me when you're done."

"Thanks, Plato." Sephie turned to Odo. "When I was scanning Plato's brain I found something odd, a large frontal lobe that's completely dark, no brainwaves. I've never seen anything like it."

"Is it brain damage? Or maybe when they created the bioforms they didn't need to use the whole brain for the engineered intelligence?"

"There's something else. It's troubling."

"What?"

"I found hidden memories, old ones. Plato has been a Five Digit for a lot longer than he thinks he has, at least ten or fifteen years. I know for certain he didn't just start here three days ago."

Odo frowned. "He has amnesia? Maybe he was in an accident and his brain was damaged."

"It's possible, but I think there's something else going on, something not good."

"We can't trick him into giving us a tour of the

tracking facility. If he gets caught, he's toast. The Single Digits will vaporize him for not turning us in."

"Are you saying you're worried about your new giant alien spider friend?"

"It's not right to take advantage of him. He seems really nice, and I don't want anything to happen to him because of us."

Silas nodded. "Odo's right, we can't take advantage of him. He trusts us. Is there another way we can take down the ConWatches?"

Sephie thought for a moment, "There might be, but it's a lot more dangerous."

Odo glanced over at Plato, then back to Sephie. "Fine, what's your ridiculously dangerous plan?"

Chapter 33

PIF

Nokk turned to Elia. "I remembered something that might be important. It just popped into my head."

"What?"

"It was a story my brother Drakk told me when I was about twelve years old. He used to sneak around at night with his friends and explore the palace, looking for secret passages and hidden rooms. The guards all knew about it, but they never stopped him because he was the emperor's son.

"One night he was snooping around the servants' quarters and they found a set of old elevator doors behind a loose wooden wall panel. He said they pried the doors open and shined a light down the shaft. The bottom was thirty feet below, and they could see a dim light coming in through a narrow gap in the wall. They decided to slide down the elevator cables and investigate."

"What did they find?"

"It was an old utility tunnel used by the workers when the palace was being built. The lights in the tunnel were dim and flickering, but it was bright enough for them to see, so they kept going. He said they walked for about two minutes, stopping when they found a big rusty iron door. My brother pressed his ear against it and heard something."

"What did he hear?"

"He said it was a strange gurgling noise, and he heard something moving."

"What did they do?"

"His friend wanted to leave, but Drakk didn't. They managed to raise the iron lever and open the door just enough to shine their light in. They could see a big metal room, a heavily armored door on the far wall. The door looked new, with two rows of blinking red lights. My brother's friend poked his head into the room, peeking behind the door to see what was making the gurgling noise. He screamed when something grabbed him, dragging him into the metal room, the iron door slamming shut."

"What did Drakk do?"

"He ran away, climbed back up the elevator shaft and didn't tell anyone what had happened."

"He just left his friend there?"

"That's what he does, that's the kind of person he is. This is where it gets spooky. His friend came to school the next day, but had no memory of the night before. He had scratches on his arms, but no idea how he got them. I used to have nightmares about it, scared the gurgling thing would come into my room and get me."

"That's beyond creepy, but how does it help us?"

"I think Drakk discovered the entrance to the underground Quantum Event Tracking facility."

"The armored door with the red lights?"

Nokk nodded. "Exactly. We need to find that door. I'm certain that's where we'll find Odo and the others. The hard part is going to be getting past the guards and into the palace. They'll have their chip scanners and bi-optic recognition systems on line."

"I wish I knew exactly where the third portal will take us."

"Can you use AR to make us disguises?"

"A big black cloak and dark glasses?"

Nokk grinned. "Maybe something a little less obvious."

"No one ever notices servants."

"Brilliant, that could work. Servants wear maroon hooded jumpsuits and keep their heads down. They're not allowed to speak or make eye contact with anyone above their palace grade level."

"That's horrible."

"And another reason why I'll never go back there."

Ten minutes later Nokk and Elia were wearing matching maroon hooded jumpsuits. "We need cleaning supplies, maybe some dust beamers?"

"Good idea." Elia tapped her wristband and two gleaming silver dust beamers appeared.

"How do these things work?"

"Hold down this tab and push it like an old fashioned broom. It turns dirt and grime into harmless vapor but doesn't damage the floor."

"Don't forget to keep your head down, and don't make eye contact or talk to anyone."

They stepped over to the third portal. "Are you ready?"

"I was born ready."

"Odo would be proud of you."

They touched the shimmering blue orb, vanishing in a blink of white light.

Nokk knew exactly where they were when he saw the shining emerald green marble floor covered with glowing gold speckles. He whispered, "We're in the palace rotunda. Guards are stationed over there at the main entrance."

Elia glanced cautiously around the room while pushing her dust beamer across the marble floor. The rotunda was huge, a steady stream of people coming and going through the circle of shimmering portals that surrounded the cavernous antechamber. She studied the guard station at the palace entrance. Nokk was right, people were being chip scanned before they were allowed to enter the palace. That was not good, they'd be identified instantly. There was only one way in, they would have to use PIFs. It was risky, but it was their only option. She moved closer to Nokk, whispering, "Hallway. Follow me."

The two friends moved slowly through the crowd, keeping their heads down, eyes on the floor, pushing the dust beamers across the rotunda.

Nokk had visited the Hall of Emperors many times when he lived in the palace, and was familiar with the long row of alcoves, each holding a fifteen-foot tall marble statue of a past emperor. When they were halfway down the curved hallway, Elia stepped into one of the alcoves, pulling Nokk in after her.

"We have to use a PIF."

"A what?"

"It's a PIF, Personal Invisibility Field. It's a secret project I helped develop for the military."

"Really? An invisibility field?"

"It's real, and it works, but it's risky. No one can see you, but people can still bump into you."

"What about their thermal scanners?"

"The PIF hides your heat and bioptic signatures."

Two wide black bracelets appeared in her hand. "Put this on your wrist. Press the violet button to activate the PIF, press the yellow one to shut it down. The invisibility field lasts for five minutes, then shuts off for ten minutes while it recharges."

"How does it work? What's the science?"

"It surrounds you with an egg-shaped energy field. Light hits it, circles around the field and comes out the opposite side. Because no light is reflecting off you, you're invisible from all directions."

223

"It really works?"

"It does. The military has been using it for about ten years."

"How do we get through the crowd of people without bumping into someone?"

"I'll create a distraction. Once it starts, we run across the rotunda and through the guard station. As soon as we're in the palace we'll have to find a place to hide so the PIFs can recharge."

"I know a good hiding spot."

"Perfect. Okay, I'm going to use AR to create a distraction. There's going to be total chaos for a minute or two, everyone running out of the rotunda."

"What are you going to do?"

"Just a little AR trick I picked up in Pangaea."

They headed back down the hallway to the rotunda, Elia saying, "Don't forget, press the violet tab to activate the PIF. You'll be able to see where you're going, but no one else can see you. Make sure no one bumps into you."

Nokk gave a start when the colossal T-rex appeared out of nowhere, letting out a thundering roar that shook the walls of the rotunda. The chaos was sudden and complete, a cacophony of terrified screams reverberating through the cavernous chamber, the crowd scrambling wildly for the exits, the doors jammed with people pushing and shoving each other trying to escape from the terrifying prehistoric beast.

Elia pressed the violet tab and disappeared, Nokk

activating his PIF seconds later.

"Head for the guard station! Follow the T-rex!"

The two friends ran behind the titanic beast as it crossed the marble floor, heading for the palace entrance. The terrified guards had ducked down behind the scanning station, Nokk and Elia racing past them into the palace.

"Go straight, the fourth door on the right is a storage room. We can hide there."

Chapter 34

Captured

Odo eyed Sephie. "What's your dangerous plan? We fight our way past five thousand giant alien spiders?"

"It's worse than that. Our goal is to shut down the tracking center and get everyone to destroy their Con-Watches, right?"

"Right."

"The problem is, there's no way I can manipulate the thoughts of fifteen thousand spiders. Cyra taught me to manipulate a group of twenty or thirty people, but not fifteen thousand."

"So your plan is…"

"We have to find another way to manipulate their thoughts."

"Which is…"

"You're not going to like it."

"You're right, I don't know what it is and I already don't like it."

"I only have to manipulate the thoughts of one spider."

Odo's eyes narrowed. "Which spider?"

"Number 1, the Single Digit in charge of the tracking facility. I'll implant false memories and he'll command all fifteen thousand spiders to send out warning messages about the ConWatches, ordering everyone to destroy their watches."

"That sounds close to completely impossible. Plato said the Single Digits have their own heavily guarded quarters. How do we get in?"

"You're really not going to like this part."

"How many parts are there that I'm not going to like?"

"Just two. Plato is going to turn us in, tell the Single Digits we're dangerous alien spies from the planet Earth."

Odo gaped at her. "Super good plan if you're trying to get us killed."

"They won't hurt us. They'll want to know why we're here and what we want."

Emmy said, "We could say Earth is planning to invade Varania. They would have a lot of questions about that."

Silas added, "And we could say we think the invasion is a bad idea, but they ordered us to come here and scout out the planet, see what kind of defenses they have."

"Nice, they'll think we're on their side."

Sephie said, "I like it, that's our plan. I'll erase Plato's memories of us and have him take us prisoner."

Odo said, "No, don't make him forget us. I have a

better idea."

"What is it?"

Odo tapped Plato. "Plato, can you hear me?"

"I hear you, my auditory sensors are functioning again."

"We have something to tell you."

"What?"

"You were right, we're intruders. We're spies from the planet Earth sent here to scout out Varania for a possible invasion. You need to turn us in to Single Digit 1. You'll be a hero, they'll probably make you a Three Digit."

"You don't seem like dangerous spies. You've been nice to me, gave me a special name and said I could keep it. The Single Digits are scary. I've heard stories about them. You won't like them."

"The truth is, we don't think Earth should invade Varania. We want to tell Single Digit 1 about the invasion plans."

"He won't be mad at you?"

"He'll probably thank us, maybe give us a medal."

"I guess I could turn you in if you really want me to."

"Thanks, Plato. It's the right thing to do."

"I need to check something first." Plato stepped over to the control console, tapping a button, a blue hologram popping up. "I'm looking up the protocol for captured intruders. It says if the intruders don't appear to be dangerous I should walk them down to the Single Digit quarters and turn them in there."

"Perfect. Lead the way, Plato. You'll be a Three Digit in no time."

The group of friends followed Plato out the door and down a long brightly lit corridor lined with floor to ceiling windows. Odo stopped, gazing down at the sprawling dome floor, five thousand spiders seated at small cylindrical consoles, furiously tapping on multicolored holographic screens. "That's incredible. Look how many spiders there are."

Plato said, "What's a spider?"

"Oh, um… that's what we call technicians on Earth. We call them spiders."

Sephie stopped, putting one hand on the window, studying the crowded dome floor.

"What are you doing?"

"I'll tell you later. Let's go."

They strolled on down the corridor, Odo spotting two large spiders standing guard at a pair of silver doors. "They have beam weapons."

Plato approached the armed guards.

"74692 on Official Level One business."

One of the spiders laughed. "A Five Digit on Level One business? Hit the road, fiver."

"These are alien intruders trying to prevent an invasion of Varania. Shall I inform Single Digit 1 that you ignored their warning? He will hold you personally responsible for the invasion of Varania."

The guard stared at him. "They don't look

229

dangerous."

Emmy floated up off the ground.

Sephie drew two quick symbols in the air, a beam weapon appearing in her hand.

The spider took a step back, the silver doors whirring open. He called out, "Five Digit 74692 on Level One business, clearance granted. Follow the light, fiver."

The armed spiders moved aside, the friends stepping into the elevator, the car descending rapidly.

Odo grinned at Plato. "Nice job with those guards. Well done."

"It was fun, quite exhilarating."

They stepped out of the elevator into a dimly lit corridor, three large spiders strolling past them. Odo's eyes were on the golden glowing orb floating in front of them.

"What's that orb?"

"I think that's the light we're supposed to follow."

They headed down the hall, the light orb drifting along in front of them.

"I guess we go down this corridor."

The adventurers wove their way through a complex maze of rooms and hallways for almost twenty minutes, passing a small group of spiders.

Plato whispered, "Those are Two Digits. Aren't they amazing?"

"They didn't seem to notice us. That's kind of weird."

Sephie nodded. "It is odd. You'd think a Two Digit would stop us and ask who we are."

"Unless they already know."

"You think they're all connected through a network?"

"It's possible."

Plato stopped, pointing down the corridor to a brightly lit glass wall. His voice was hushed, almost reverent. "Single Digits."

The glowing orb led them to the glass wall, Odo studying the two enormous spiders sleeping on immense plush purple velvet pads. The walls were gleaming gold, silver tables laden down with all manner of fresh fruits and vegetables, crystal vases filled with brightly colored flowers.

Plato whispered, "Look at all the food. I've never seen anything like it. It looks so delicious."

"Those are Single Digits?"

"Yes. This is exactly how my friend described it. Aren't they amazing? Just look at them."

Odo was getting a strange feeling. "They don't look very busy."

"The orb is moving. We go through that door."

Sephie said, "Don't forget, we don't talk to anyone but Single Digit 1. While you're telling him about the invasion, I'll be doing what I have to do."

"Got it."

The friends stepped into a circular gold room, the door whirring shut behind them, the light orb vanishing.

Silas scanned the interior of the room. "I don't see any doors. How do we get to the Single Digit quarters?"

"I don't know."

"I guess we wait for them."

Sephie was getting a bad feeling. "I don't like this. Something is wrong."

Chapter 35

The Iron Door

Nokk and Elia darted into the storage room, closing the door behind them.

"We did it, we're in the palace."

"Those PIFs are amazing. You really helped develop them?"

"I was being modest; I designed them myself."

"You're amazing. I made this little antigravity ring, but it's really just a new use for existing tech."

"Most inventions combine old tech to make new tech. Now you're being modest."

Nokk grinned. "I am kind of proud of it. You should have seen the look on Odo's face when I lifted a big table with one hand."

"Show off."

"I don't know why I did it. I guess I wanted to impress someone. People made fun of me when I was growing up."

"Why?"

"Because of my height."

"We're the same height. Are you going to make fun of me?"

"Of course not. You're amazing. You're an AR engineer and a brilliant inventor."

"I'm not very strong though."

"That doesn't matter, you're amazing."

Elia grinned at him, raising her eyebrows.

"Oh, I see what you did there. You made me say it doesn't matter how tall or how strong you are."

"Consider me impressed."

"Thanks. Now we just have to find the others and shut down the tracking facility."

"We'll figure something out. Hey, maybe when this is all over Odo and Sephie will let us join the Odd Squad."

"We'd need superhero names."

"I suppose we should save the world first, then think up our names."

"Agreed. The servants' quarters are on the level below us. There's a back stairway about a hundred feet down the hall. We can take that instead of the main stairs, it will be safer. It should only take us about three minutes to get to the servants' quarters."

"That should give us enough time. The PIFs are fully charged."

The two friends stepped out into the gleaming marble hallway, Elia studying the long row of exquisitely carved marble statues.

"Someone likes statues."

Nokk grinned, keeping his head down as he pushed the dust beamer in front of him. "It's an emperor thing. They all do it."

"I guess they don't want to be forgotten."

"Good luck with that. The stairway is in here." Nokk stepped into an alcove, heading down a narrow spiral staircase.

When they reached the bottom, Elia peered out into a crowded hallway. "Activate your PIF. It's busy down here, so be careful not to bump into anyone. Which way?"

"We go left."

They dodged through the crowd, Nokk whispering, "Servants' quarters are at the end of the corridor past the banquet hall. It must be mealtime, it's crowded."

"Only a minute left on the PIFs. We're going to need a place to hide."

"Third door down is a storage room. We can go in there."

They hurried down the hall past a group of servants, stepping into the small room. Nokk froze when he saw the guard sitting in a chair having his lunch. It was too late, their PIFs blinked off, the guard gaping at them.

"How did you–" He stopped, his eyes widening. "You! You're supposed to be dead!"

It was almost a reflex now, the rippling time orb shooting out of Nokk's hand, the look of surprise on the guard's face just before he vanished.

Nokk looked at Elia. "I had to do it."

"I know you did. How far did you send him?"

"Two or three days, I think. It happened so fast."

"He'll be fine. He recognized you, even with your servant's uniform. He'll tell everyone he saw you when he gets back."

"I know. We have to hurry."

"How are we going to shut down the tracking facility?"

"I'm thinking a couple of heavy particle beam blasters should do nicely. We can vaporize the machine."

"I like the way you think."

"We'll use the PIFs, but if we get into trouble you'll have to hit them with a time orb."

"You could create an AR distraction."

"Let's try stealth first. The last thing we need is a bunch of palace guards running around here."

"Good point."

They activated their PIFs, heading down the hall to the servants' quarters. Nokk peered in, whispering, "We're in luck, it's almost empty. The elevator doors are on the back wall behind a dark green wood panel."

"There it is, just past that row of beds."

Nokk darted over to the panel. "How do we get it off?"

A metal pry bar appeared in Elia's hands.

"Love that AR." Nokk grabbed it, gently separating the panel from the wall. "Bingo, elevator doors." He pried them open, eyeing the dangling elevator cables. "I guess that's our way down."

Elia whispered, "Let's go."

They slipped through the opening, Nokk pulling the elevator doors shut behind him, the two friends shimmying down the cables to the utility tunnel below.

"No lights down here. My brother said there were lights."

A glowing orb appeared in Elia's hand, the light casting long eerie flickering shadows. "Which way?"

"We go left, keep walking until we find an old rusty iron door."

"Then we listen for a horrible gurgling noise?"

Nokk grimaced. "That was a long time ago. Whatever it was is gone by now."

"I'll let you peek behind the door just to make sure."

"Thanks. How are those particle beam blasters coming along? I might need one."

They crept down the utility tunnel, Elia spotting the iron door. "That's really creepy. Do you think this used to be a dungeon?"

"Maybe. We've had some pretty strange emperors since the palace was built." Nokk pressed his ear against the door. "Hold on, I hear someone sharpening a giant axe."

"Nice try. You go first."

Nokk raised the heavy iron lever, the door squealing open. He yelped when he saw the huge spider filling a bucket from a gurgling spigot, it's eight eyes suddenly glowing with a brilliant orange light. The spider was fast, but Nokk was faster, the creature vanishing in a rippling time orb.

"What was that?"

"That must have been what grabbed Drakk's friend."

"Do you think it was a bioform?"

"I'm not sure. I feel like I've seen one before, but I don't know where."

"You can't remember where you saw a giant spider with orange glowing eyes? It's kind of hard to forget something like that."

"I know, it is odd. It's almost like I dreamed about it or something."

Nokk pointed to the heavily armored door and its two rows of small blinking red lights. "That looks like the entrance to something very special."

"Like a top secret Quantum Event Tracking System?"

Nokk grinned. "Lucky guess. Let's find out. How do we get past it?"

Elia tapped her wristband and six-foot long particle beam weapon on a heavy tripod appeared in front of the door.

"Excellent, you found the key."

Elia stepped behind the deadly weapon. "As Odo would say, *it's showtime.*"

Chapter 36

Escape

Silas was slumped on the floor, leaning back against the gold metallic wall. "I don't think anyone is coming."

"Plato, can you communicate with your friends?"

"I cannot, I receive all my commands directly from a Four Digit."

"You're not all linked together?"

"No."

"Do have any idea why the Single Digits aren't here yet?"

"It's possible they have been watching you since you arrived and we are now their prisoners. I have heard stories of their amazing powers of perception."

Odo frowned. "They didn't look very amazing. They were just lying around sleeping on those big velvet beds."

Sephie said, "It's time to get out of here. Odo, would you like to show us how it's done?"

Odo got to his feet. "The incredible Translucent Boy will once again save the day." He pressed his hand against the wall. Five seconds later nothing had happened. "It's not working. I can't make a door."

Sephie was drawing a symbol in the air when a chilling voice filled the room.

"Such curious little creatures. What in the world were you hoping to accomplish?"

Odo called out, "We're here to warn you about an invasion."

"Oh, dear. Are your little Earth friends going to come to Varania and throw rocks at us? Such a terrifying thought. What ever shall we do?"

"You know we're from Earth?"

"Your little Five Digit friend was quite right, we've been watching and listening to you since you arrived. Did you really think you could destroy the Quantum Event Tracking System? Take down an emperor? Destroy my ConWatches? You are pitiful little children. I would send you home, but sadly you know too much for me to let you live. I have pressing matters at the moment, but I'll get back to you. Try to enjoy your last few hours in this world. Ta ta!"

The friends stared at each other.

"We have to get out of here. That guy is nuts."

"Plato, was that a Single Digit?"

"I don't believe so. I'm quite certain it was one of our creators, a Varanian."

Odo said, "I think it was the emperor. He called them *my* ConWatches. And he sounded crazy enough to be an emperor."

Sephie drew four symbols in the air, a powerful Plindorian beam pistol appearing in her hand. "Let's try this." She aimed it at the doorway, pressing the tab, a brilliant beam of purple light shooting out.

"It's not doing anything. It should vaporize it."

Silas said, "These are definitely not ordinary walls. They're absorbing the beam's energy."

Emmy said, "Maybe they're AR, like the buildings in Pangaea."

"They must be. They're not made of matter, so they're not affected by Odo's translucent power or the beam gun."

"We're trapped here?"

"There has to be a way out. There has to be."

"I wish Elia was here. She could use her AR to get us out."

The room was quiet until Sephie whispered, "Bingo."

Odo scooted over next to her. "What is it?"

"Shh." She drew a symbol in the air, a small piece of folded paper appearing in Odo's hand. He opened it carefully, read it, then folded it up again, a broad grin on his face. He leaned over and kissed Sephie on the cheek.

Odo handed the piece of paper to Silas.

Silas read it, handing it to Emmy. "Well done!"

Sephie turned to Odo. "Let's rock and roll, boys."

Odo pressed his hand against the ancient stone floor, a shimmering doorway appearing. "We're good, there's a tunnel below us."

Odo was the last one down, the translucent doorway vanishing, the stone floor solid again.

Plato said, "A very imaginative solution. Very clever."

"Thanks, Plato. I'd like to see the look on that crazy emperor's face when he comes back and finds us gone."

Sephie said, "I keep getting a feeling that there's something we're missing, but I don't know what it is."

"Does anyone else think there was something really odd about the Single Digits?"

Silas nodded. "Why would they have a clear glass wall? Why would they want the other spiders to watch them eat fruits and veggies, sleep on giant cushy beds?"

"And if they were in charge of the tracking center they wouldn't be lying around on big pillows eating snacks and sleeping all day, they'd be busy working."

Emmy said, "It kind of reminded me of a museum display, a diorama."

"That's it! That's exactly what it's like! I think it's all for show, maybe to keep the spiders working, keep them hoping that one day they'll be a Single Digit and can just lie around and eat snacks."

Silas nudged Emmy, whispering loudly, "Like Odo does."

She laughed. "Good one."

"I'm going to ignore that. Here's a question, if the Single Digits aren't running the tracking center, then who is?"

Sephie said, "I don't think it's the emperor, he's too busy being crazy and building statues of himself."

Emmy nodded her agreement. "Definitely not him."

Silas was rubbing his chin. "The room we were held captive in has the same AR gold walls as the Single Digit quarters."

"You're saying the Single Digits are AR? They aren't real?"

"It would make sense. Like Emmy said, it's just a diorama for the other spiders to see, a way to motivate them."

"Maybe there's something important hidden behind the display."

"How do we get to it?"

Plato said, "Perhaps you could go up through the ceiling, the same way you escaped from the AR room."

"Good idea. We just have to figure out exactly where to go up."

Odo crouched down on the floor, drawing a diagram in the dust with his finger. "The room we were in is here, and the Single Digit quarters was over here. We have to go in this direction for maybe a hundred feet or so, then go up through the ceiling."

"There's a side passage up ahead we can take. I wish we had a map so we knew exactly where to go. The emperor will have a billion guards looking for us once he finds out we're missing."

"Hopefully he won't know we're down in these

creepy old tunnels."

They headed into the side passageway, Odo peering into the darkness. "It looks kind of spooky down there. There's probably a bunch of skeleton warriors with swords and axes."

Silas laughed. "I like it. If only we had a magic shield."

Sephie flicked her wrist, an orb of bright light appearing in front of them. "How's that?"

"Much better than a magic shield. Not a skeleton warrior in sight."

The friends headed down the narrow tunnel, Odo counting his steps.

"This is about a hundred feet. It we go straight up we should be behind the Single Digit quarters."

"What do you think is up there?"

"I have no idea, but we'll have to be ready for anything."

Sephie drew three symbols in the air, a wooden ladder blinking into existence. "We can use this to get up there."

Odo climbed the narrow ladder, pressing his hand against the stone ceiling, a shimmering doorway appearing. He poked his head through, then pulled it back, a look of horror on his face.

Chapter 37

The Queen

Silas' eyes were wide. "What did you see up there?"

"Shhh! Footsteps! Someone's out there."

The friends ducked down, Odo whispering, "Do you think it's the emperor's guards?"

Sephie drew a symbol, the light orb blinking off.

Emmy whispered, "It's dark here. So spooky."

Silas whispered, "Did you hear that clinking sound? It sounded like skeleton warriors dragging their swords."

"Ha ha."

Sephie said, "I'm going to use the Traveling Eye and look around." She sat on the floor, closing her eyes, her consciousness drifting out of her body. She floated straight up through the floor, then back down again. She shivered when she saw what Odo had seen, understanding the look on his face. Floating down the narrow passage to the main tunnel, she turned left, listening for footsteps.

She took two more turns, stopping when she saw them.

Twenty seconds later she was back in her body, her eyes opening. "Follow me! Hurry!"

"What is it, what did you see?"

"Hurry!" She ran down the passageway, the others right behind her. Two minutes later they were racing down a wide tunnel when Silas screeched to a halt, Odo crashing into him, the two of them tumbling to the ground.

"Why did you stop?"

Emmy gave a shout. "It's Nokk and Elia! They're here! They found us!"

Odo jumped up, spotting Nokk and Elia standing next to a heavy beam weapon on a tripod. He waved to them as he raced down the tunnel.

"You're safe! How did you find us? Did you come through the portal after us?"

Elia said, "We found another portal that took us to the royal palace, then we came down an old elevator shaft that Nokk's brother Drakk found when they were children."

"We're under the royal palace?"

Nokk said, "We are. That's where the tracking center is."

Elia gave a start when she spotted Plato. "What is that?"

"This is our friend Plato. He's a Five Digit."

"A what?"

The friends traded stories for almost an hour, Odo

explaining how the spiders track the ConWatches and send out the messages, Nokk telling them about the PIFs and how they had gotten past the palace guards using the AR T-rex.

Elia couldn't take her eyes off Plato. "You're absolutely certain you're a bioform?"

"We were created by the Varanians to track the ConWatches."

Nokk slapped his palm to his forehead. "I know where I've seen you! It was when I was very small, two or three years old. I was in the throne room and saw my father talking to someone who looks exactly like you."

Elia gave a yelp. "They're Argonians! I read about them in school. You're not a bioform, you're a living creature from a distant world, from Argonia."

"I'm quite certain we were created by the Varanians."

"No, they lied to you. You're not a bioform, you're an Argonian. You have no memory of your past?"

"My only memory is being a Five Digit."

Sephie said, "When I scanned your brain, your prefrontal lobe was dark, completely inactive. They deactivated your memories and lied to you, told you they had created you."

Emmy gaped at Plato. "They're slaves?"

Nokk said, "I can't believe my father would do something like this. I know he's ruthless, but this doesn't seem like him."

Odo said, "I saw something when I looked through

the ceiling. It was awful, but I think I know how the Argonians are being controlled."

Sephie said, "I saw it too. It was dreadful."

"You need to show us. We tried to blast a hole in this door with the beam weapon, but there's an energy shield around it. It will take us hours to get through it."

"We know a quick way to get there."

The friends wove their way back through the shadowy tunnels, arriving at the narrow side passageway.

"It's right above us."

Odo climbed up the ladder, pressing his hand against the ceiling, a shimmering doorway appearing.

Emmy said, "Take my hand and I'll fly everyone up."

Three minutes later the friends had the same look they had seen on Odo's face.

"It's a gigantic spider, but what are all those cables and tubes going into it? What are all those machines next to it?"

Emmy whispered, "It's huge. It must be thirty feet long."

"Is it alive?"

Silas said, "I saw one of its legs move. It's alive."

"That's horrible. What are they doing to it?"

Sephie scanned the gargantuan spider's brain waves. "It has the same brain mapping as Plato, and its prefrontal lobe is dark, just like his."

Elia said, "I think it's the Argonian queen. I think they're using her mind to control the workers."

"How do we free her?"

Elia stepped over to one of the pulsating machines, studying it. "They're feeding her through this machine. These others are connected to her nervous system, circulatory system and to her brain."

"What do we do?"

Elia was about to reply when two sets of doors slid open, a dozen armed guards streaming into the huge circular room. One of them hollered, "Back away from her!"

Nokk stepped forward. "You don't recognize your old pal Little Nokky?"

A murmur ran through the guards.

"Prince Nokk is dead. The emperor killed him."

Nokk stepped closer.

"It's him, it's Prince Nokk!"

"He's a mutant. Kill him!"

Nokk held up one hand. "Before you kill me, I'd like to introduce a few friends of mine. They call themselves the Odd Squad."

Sephie drew a quick symbol, a powerful shimmering energy shield appearing in front of them. Emmy floated up into the air.

One of the guards fired his weapon at Sephie, the blast of purple light bouncing harmlessly off the wall of energy.

Nokk extended one arm, a time orb shooting across the room, the captain of the guard vanishing.

Elia tapped her wristband, twenty heavily armed AR warriors appearing.

The palace guards turned and ran, the doors closing behind them.

Odo stared at Elia's warriors. "Whoa, who are those guys?"

Elia laughed. "They just look scary, they don't actually do anything."

"The guards will be back. The emperor will send a thousand troops if he has to."

Elia studied the machines. "All the cables and tubes are AR. I can make them go away."

Sephie said, "Wait, I want to try something. I might be able to reconnect her prefrontal lobe, reactivate her memories."

"We don't have much time."

Sephie ran over to the gigantic spider, pressing her hands against it. She closed her eyes, her consciousness leaving her body, floating inside the spider's body. She found its brain, moving toward the dark prefrontal lobe. "That's how they did it, they bypassed the memory lobe with that synthetic neuronic bundle. The memory lobe doesn't look damaged." A beam of white hot energy shot out from her ghostly hand, the bundle of synthetic neurons vanishing, the prefrontal lobe now glowing brightly. "That's it, her memories are back online."

She flashed out of the spider's body into her own. "It's done, I restored her memories."

Elia stepped over to the wall of machines, tapping her wristband. Seconds later the machines, the cables and tubes were gone, all eight of the enormous spider's eyes blinking open.

Chapter 38

Golden Doors

The spider's voice was soft, almost melodic. "What is this place? I remember the ships arriving, landing near our village, seeing the soldiers, but nothing after that." She gazed down at Plato, studying him. "You are one of mine. I will help you remember."

Sephie scanned Plato's brain waves, watching as his dark memory lobe flared brightly.

Plato shivered, then said, "I remember everything! They took us, took all of us into the ship. They didn't create us, they took us from our home. There was blackness, and then this world. There are others here. Thousands of us."

"I can feel them all. They are my children, and they are lost."

"Can you make them remember? Can you free them?"

"Soon. My strength is growing, returning to me, but I need time to fully recover."

Elia said, "We need to find the emperor. We have to finish this."

Nokk's eyes were on the mammoth spider. "I can't believe my father would do this."

Odo said, "Do you know where he is? We could talk to him. Make him listen to us."

Nokk's face was grim. "The time for talk is over. His reign as emperor is over." He headed through a pair of silver doors, the others following him.

A dozen guards were standing at the end of the marble hallway, beam weapons glowing brightly. They never had a chance, the shimmering time orb hitting them before they realized what was happening.

Nokk ran towards a set of wide marble stairs. "Up these stairs and turn right, then one more set of stairs."

Elia grabbed his arm. "We should slow down, we don't know what kind of defenses the emperor has. There might be AR engineers waiting for us, or android warriors."

"You're right. I just want this to be over, to send the Argonians home, destroy the ConWatches."

"We'll fix this, but we have to be careful."

Sephie said, "I can use the Traveling Eye to scout out their defenses."

"Let's try this instead." Elia tapped her wristband, a PIF appearing in her hand. She handed it to Nokk. "Take this. If you see anything, hit it with a time orb."

Odo said, "What is that thing?"

"It's called a PIF, a Personal Invisibility Field."

Nokk slapped it onto his wrist. "Wait here." He tapped

the violet button, vanishing.

Silas grinned. "So cool. I wish I had one."

Odo could hear Nokk running up the stairs. There were shouts, then bright flashes of light, then silence.

"What happened?"

"Is he all right?"

Footsteps sounded, Nokk staggering into view, half his left arm missing, one side of him blackened from a beam blast. He was bleeding badly. "They had scanners, they could see me. They're gone now."

Elia ran over to him. "Your arm!"

Nokk sank to his knees. "I'm getting weak."

Elia pressed her hands to his chest, closing her eyes, the others watching as the bleeding stopped, the dreadful burns fading away, his arm reforming. She let go of him. "You're good. All better."

Nokk stared at his arm. "What kind of AR was that? I've never seen anything like it. How did you do that?"

Elia hesitated, then said, "It wasn't AR. It was something else."

"What was it?"

"It's something I can do."

"I don't understand. It's not AR?"

"I'm a healer. A mutant."

"Why didn't you tell us?"

"Old habits. I would have been put to death if anyone knew. Even my parents didn't know. I healed my mom after the accident. She was alone in her room, in a coma.

She was dying and I brought her back, but I never told anyone."

"You saved my life."

"How many soldiers were there?"

"Twenty or thirty, and four android warriors. They'll be back in a month or two."

"Lead the way."

The group of friends headed up the stairs, turning right, heading down a wide corridor lined with marble statues, the curved ceiling painted to resemble a summer sky with puffy white clouds.

Odo studied it. "The clouds are moving!"

Elia nodded. "It's AR."

They strode down the hall, reaching the second set of stairs. Nokk peered around the corner then jumped back. "Sephie, can you make an energy shield?"

She drew a symbol, a wavering wall of energy appearing across the stairway. "That should stop just about anything."

Nokk stepped in front of the stairs, soldiers shouting a warning, a dozen deadly beams bouncing off the wall of energy. He extended both arms, two enormous roiling time orbs shooting up the stairs. The shouting stopped.

The energy shield blinked off, Nokk stepping silently up the stairs, peering around the corner. "All clear. The throne room is at the end of this hallway."

The others ran up the stairs after him.

Elia held up one hand. "Wait!" She tapped her

wristband, three AR android warriors appearing. "Run down the hall to the doors."

They watched as the AR androids raced across the marble floor, heading toward the emperor's throne room. They had almost reached the massive gold doors when a blast of red light hit them.

Elia tapped her wristband, the AR androids vanishing. "There are soldiers in a side passageway with an anti-matter weapon. Sephie's energy shield won't protect us against that."

"They have scanners."

Emmy said, "On the ceiling?"

"What do you mean?"

Emmy pressed her hands against one of the massive marble statues, floating it up in the air.

"What are you doing?"

"I thought I'd pay them a little visit. Drop in unannounced." She floated up to the ceiling, her ghostly form drifting down the corridor. She turned into the side passageway, the fifteen-foot tall marble statue directly above the black antimatter gun.

Odo heard a terrific crash, then shouting. Emmy flew out of the passageway and down the hall, landing in front of them. "No more antimatter gun. It got crushed by an emperor who didn't want to be forgotten."

Silas cheered. "Way to go, Dream Girl!"

"How many soldiers are there?"

"About a dozen, and they're heavily armed. I could

fly you down there, but you'd have to be quick."

"I could hit them with a time orb."

"You'll turn solid when I let go of you. You'll have to send out the orb as you're falling, before they fire their weapons."

"Let's do it."

Elia grabbed his arm. "Please be careful."

"I will, I promise."

Emmy took Nokk's hand, floating him up to the ceiling. Odo watched as they drifted silently down the hallway, stopping when they reached the side passageway. A few seconds later Emmy let go of Nokk's hand. As he was falling, a massive time orb shot down the passageway. He hit the ground, rolling to one side, then stood up.

"We're good!"

Emmy floated back down, her physical body returning.

The others raced down the hall, joining Nokk in front of the golden doors.

"The emperor is in there."

Elia said, "But what kind of defenses does he have? There must be soldiers, more androids."

"I'll check." Sephie closed her eyes, her consciousness leaving her body. She drifted through the golden doors. There was only one person in the room, and he was seated on the throne, his eyes focused on the golden doors.

Sephie returned to her physical body. "No soldiers, no

androids. The emperor is on the throne. I think he's wait-ing for us."

Nokk tapped a silver disk on the wall, the golden doors silently opening.

Chapter 39

Drakk

Nokk stepped into the throne room, the others right behind him. The man on the throne gave a cold smile.

"Well, isn't this a surprise, it's Little Nokky, back from the dead. It would seem our father was far weaker than I had imagined. He should have killed you when he had the chance."

Nokk stared at his brother. "Where is the emperor? Where is our father?"

"Our father is far, far away, but the emperor is sitting on the throne."

"You're the emperor? What did you do to our father?"

"Oh, my, are you upset? You look upset. I gave him two choices, and he chose the second one. He's living in exile on a very distant world. He willfully and freely abdicated his role as the emperor of Varania."

"What was the first choice you gave him?"

"It was quite dreadful, I assure you, and involved a lot of his friends and family."

Nokk's face was dark. "Your reign as emperor is

going to be a short one. It ends today."

"You are an industrious little fellow, aren't you? Claiming your rightful place on the throne and attempting to destroy the Quantum Event Tracking System all in one day. Such a busy little boy."

Nokk turned the others. "I'd like you to meet my brother Drakk. This is his last day as emperor of Varania. He's the one who discovered the entrance to the tracking center."

"Did you know the duke's son was going to kill you?"

"I knew it. I could see it in his eyes."

"But did you know I paid him quite handsomely to kill you? He failed and he paid dearly for his ineptitude."

Nokk took a step back. "You hired him to kill your own brother? Who are you? What are you?"

"I'm the emperor, and you're not. And who is that lovely young lady with you? She looks very familiar. Ah, now I remember, she's the AR engineer who developed the invisibility fields. That would explain how you managed to escape the Friends of Varania. Oh, well, as they always say, if you want something done right, do it yourself."

Nokk snorted. "You have no idea who and what we are."

"Did I mention we have made some stunning modifications to your marvelous invisibility fields? It's all very high tech and top secret, but the fields are quite undetectable now and stay active for over an hour."

Elia's eyes narrowed.

Drakk clapped his hands, two dozen heavily armed soldiers suddenly appearing in front of the throne. He gave an icy smile. "Well, you tried, you did your best, and that's the important thing, isn't it? Sadly, our ways must part, and it's time for you and your little friends to move on to a far, far better place."

What happened next would be forever etched in Odo's memory. Twenty-two very angry Argonians swarmed over the balcony, dropping down onto the soldiers, spraying them with a viscous green fluid as they fell, the soldiers sinking silently to the ground.

Drakk jumped to his feet, his eyes filled with a blind maniacal rage. "There really is no end to your insolence is there? Your father would be proud of the vile creature you've become."

"He wouldn't be proud at all. I'm nothing like him, and nothing like you."

"Did I forget to mention he left you a gift, a token of his deep love for you?"

"What kind of gift?"

"I have it right here." Drakk turned around, pulling something out of a side pocket in the throne. He spun around, a gleaming gold beam gun in his hand. Much to his surprise he was greeted not by a startled Nokk, but by a very large rippling time orb. Odo would never forget the horrible sneer on Drakk's face right before he flickered and vanished.

The room was silent, the guards lying motionless on the floor. Sephie scanned their brainwaves. They were alive, but temporarily paralyzed by whatever the spiders had sprayed on them.

Nokk took Elia's hand in his. "Now I know."

"That your brother tried to have you killed?"

"Not that. I know how far I can send someone into the future. It's one thousand and twenty-nine years, give or take a few hours."

"I wonder what kind of world your brother will find there?"

"I only care about this world."

Plato said, "I'm getting a message from the queen. She says she has restored the memories of all her children and they have stopped sending out the ConWatch warnings."

"Excellent. That's a good start. We still have much to do in the tracking center. How long until the guards recover?"

Plato said, "About two hours and they'll be fully awake."

Odo eyed the sleeping guards. "What exactly was that green stuff they sprayed?"

Sephie scanned their brainwaves again. "It's affecting their hypothalamus, putting them into a deep sleep."

Thirty minutes later the friends were standing on the main floor of the Quantum Event Tracking System, the room packed with thousands of Argonians.

Nokk hopped up onto a control console, looking across the crowded floor. "To all the Argonians, I have this message. Your days as slaves of the Varanian emperor are over. All of you will soon be returning to your world through an interstellar transition portal. I thank those of you who helped to depose the emperor in the throne room. For this you have my undying gratitude. You have made Varania a better world."

Eight thousand Argonians stomped their feet, the floor shaking.

Nokk hopped down, turning to Elia. "It was you who started this chain of events, and it should be you who brings it to a close."

Elia nodded. She stepped over to the central control panel, studying it for a moment, tapping a series of buttons, a holoscreen popping up. She called out, "This will permanently disable the ConWatches." She tapped the holoscreen, a shrill alarm sounding. She tapped it again and the alarm stopped. "That's it. No more ConWatches. It's over."

"It's not quite over. Where's that heavy particle weapon you were telling me about?"

Elia tapped her wristband, a gleaming beam rifle appearing in her hands.

Nokk pointed to the wall of controls. "Would you like to do the honors?"

Elia pressed the tab, moving the brilliant beam of purple light across the dome wall, vaporizing the controls.

"No more spying on Varanian citizens, no more controlling their actions. People will live their lives as they choose, be what they want to be, be who they want to be."

An hour later they were back in the throne room, Nokk facing Odo, Sephie, Silas, and Emmy.

"None of this could have happened without you, without the Odd Squad. You have my undying thanks for everything you have done. The Odd Squad will be remembered for all time on Varania."

Silas said, "You and Elia can join the Odd Squad if you want. We're always looking for new members."

Odo stared at Silas, his eyes narrowing. He was up to something. Definitely up to something.

Elia said, "We would be proud to join your marvelous group. It would be a great honor."

Silas grinned at Odo. "It's going to be hard to keep track of all these new members. We're definitely going to need a secret handshake."

Chapter 40

Nobles

Odo turned when the elderly purple caped Varanian stepped tentatively into the throne room. "Prince Nokk? If I might have a quick word with you?"

Nokk studied the old man. "You're Counselor Erzak. You were my father's Imperial Advisor. You were always kind to me."

"How nice of you to remember. If I might ask, is your brother Drakk anywhere to be found? I had a few questions regarding his rightful status as emperor, now that you have returned."

"He should be here in about one thousand and twenty-nine years, if you'd like to wait for him."

A barely perceptible smile crossed Counselor Erzak's face. "I see. That does simplify matters, since he is no longer the rightful heir to the throne, a fact which will make a great many people quite happy. I noticed my ConWatch is no longer functioning. This is your doing?"

"Everyone here had a part in it."

"Excellent news indeed. They were a most annoying

contrivance, if I might say so, and will not be missed."

"They did not do what the emperor said they did. The warning messages were false, simply a means for him to control the behavior of the citizens."

"I thought as much, but was unable to safely voice my suspicions until now."

"I will be abdicating my role as rightful heir to the throne, if that's what you're worried about."

"Oh, dear, it's quite the opposite. I'm afraid that Varania needs your leadership now far more than you know. There is a great deal of unrest, thanks to your brother. Civil war is imminent if the throne is not claimed by a rightful heir. Many people would die, and it would be anarchy, complete chaos."

Nokk thought for a minute, then turned to Elia. "What do you think?"

"I can think of no better person to rule over Varania than you. You're precisely what they need now. Someone who is trustworthy and kind, someone who is not seeking power or wealth."

Nokk looked away for a moment, then said, "Counselor Erzak, these are my conditions; I will take the throne for a period of one year, and when that year is up, the citizens of Varania will decide whether they wish me to remain emperor for another year. I will need a minimum of six able advisors, Elia to be one of them. My first act as emperor will be disbanding the Friends of Varania, my second act will allow all genetically engineered

Varanians to live their lives without fear of persecution."

Counselor Erzak stepped over to Nokk, grasping his hand. "This might very well be the happiest day of my life, Emperor Nokk."

Odo, Sephie, Silas, and Emmy cheered, darting over to Nokk and Elia, congratulating them.

Silas said, "We have an emperor in the Odd Squad! How cool is that?"

Plato stepped into the throne room, running over to Odo. "The portal to Argonia has been activated, but the queen wants to give you something before she goes home."

"What kind of something?" Odo's eyes were bright.

Sephie said, "It's not a chest full of gold coins, Odo."

Odo rolled his eyes. "I don't need anything ridiculous like that. I'd be perfectly happy with something simple, maybe an antigrav car or my own personal android assistant. A small palace would be nice, nothing too fancy, maybe one on a big lake."

"Nice try, Odo."

The friends followed Plato down the stairs, heading out through the rotunda. Odo spotted the large blue portal in the main palace square. "Whoa, that's a big one."

Plato nodded. "There are over fifteen thousand Argonians heading home. And, not to be indelicate, but the queen is of a certain size that requires a rather substantial portal."

Odo grinned. "Well said."

They ran down the steps, the queen waving to them.

"I wanted to thank you again for your bravery and kindness. Argonia owes you so very much. This is but a small token of our deep appreciation for what you have done, but I hope it will bring you some amount of happiness. My only request is that you not open it until you return home."

Sephie said, "You don't need to give us anything. We were glad to help, that's what the Odd Squad does."

Odo jabbed her sharply with his elbow.

Sephie gave him a disapproving look, then smiled and said, "But we appreciate your generosity and promise not to open it until we get home."

The queen laughed, handing Sephie a small silver latched box, saying, "Thank you again for everything."

Plato gave each of them an awkward hug. "Perhaps we'll meet again sometime." It was the first time Odo had ever hugged a giant alien spider.

Sephie said, "I hope we see you again. You have been a true friend, Plato."

An hour later the towering portal blinked off, the Argonians gone.

Silas said, "We did it. We freed them all, dethroned an evil emperor, shut down the tracking center and the Con-Watches."

Odo nodded. "Not bad for four kids."

Emmy added, "Four kids, two Varanians, a bunch of giant spiders, some retired robots, an old paleontologist, and a crazy windshield repair guy named Ralph."

Silas laughed. "I guess we did have a little help along the way."

"I'm going to miss Plato. I never thought I'd have a giant alien spider friend."

"He probably never thought he'd have human friends."

Odo turned when he saw two palace guards in purple cloaks approaching them.

"Emperor Nokk has requested the honor of your presence in the throne room."

"For what?"

"It is not my place to say, sir."

Odo grinned. "Sir?"

"If you would follow me?"

The adventurers followed the guards back into the palace and up the stairs to the throne room.

"Do we have to call him Emperor Nokk?"

"I think so, he is the emperor."

Elia called out when they entered the room. "There they are!"

Nokk waved them over. "The Argonians have all returned to their world?"

"They have."

"Excellent. I wanted to thank you for everything you've done in my official capacity as emperor of Varania. I have spoken with my counselors and we made a unanimous decision. The four of you shall forever be

269

honored members of the Emperor's Court of Varania."

Elia handed four small boxes to Nokk, whispering to the four friends, "This part was my idea."

Nokk opened the first box, pulling out a round medallion attached to a purple and white ribbon. He hung it around Odo's neck.

Odo eyed the medallion. "This is the same medallion that Harold had. We can shift with these?"

"You can. Elia and I hope you will use them to visit us. You are always welcome, and as nobles, you each have a private room in the palace at your disposal."

"This is amazing. Of course we'll come and visit."

Elia leaned over, whispering something in Sephie's ear.

Sephie laughed. "No way will we miss that. We'll be here, just tell us when it's going to be."

Odo's eyes narrowed. "Wait, are you and Nokk getting married?"

Sephie punched his arm. "Shhh!"

Chapter 41

The Van

The four friends used a medallion to return home, turning the blue stone clockwise for three complete turns, arriving on the sidewalk in front of Harold's house.

"We should let Harold know we're back."

Odo ran up the stairs, knocking on the door. A few moments later it swung open, Harold peering out.

"Yes, may I help you?"

"It's me, Odo Whitley. We helped you to get rid of the dinosaur that was eating your food."

"Of course, now I remember. These are your friends? Please come in."

"We can't stay long, but we wanted to see how you're doing."

"I'm doing quite well, reading some of my old books. I'm a paleontologist, you know."

Odo nodded. "I know you are, a famous one. You've written a lot of books. I wanted to return this, it's the medallion your father gave you, the one he found in

Antarctica. You used it to walk to the moon."

"That must be where I got the moon rocks. Thank you so much, I was wondering where that was."

Sephie said, "Are you all set for food? Do you need anything?"

"I have all the food I need. My nephew brought me four big bags of groceries. My cupboards are full."

"Your nephew? I didn't think you had a nephew."

"I don't remember having one, but I've forgotten so many things. He was very nice, said he would stop by again to check on me. He was very impressed with my collection of prehistoric fossils and artifacts."

"Is your nephew's name Ralph?"

"I believe so, do you know him?"

"I've met him. He seems nice."

They chatted for a few more minutes, then headed home.

"That's very weird. There's no way Ralph is his nephew."

"He brought him groceries. That was thoughtful."

"I wish I knew who he was. Do you think he could be a formshifter, an alien like Mrs. Preke?"

"Maybe. He helped you when you dropped the bowling ball on your dad's car, and he's helping Harold, so he must be nice."

Odo looked skeptical. "He could be up to something. Maybe he's being friendly with Harold so he can steal all his stuff, like those dinosaur skulls."

"Not everyone is up to something, Odo."

"I know that, I just worry about Harold living there all alone, and the people who might try to take advantage of him. He gets confused, he might give someone all his money, or tell them about the moon rocks and the medallion."

"We'll check on him. If he needs help we'll get him help."

"I can stop by when I get home from school, see how he's doing."

The friends headed home, Odo running up the stairs into his house.

"Odo Whitley is in the house!"

Albert called out from the living room. "You don't have to shout. The house shook like an earthquake when you slammed the front door." He gave a loud laugh.

Odo grinned. His dad was laughing, that was good. He stepped into the living room, spotting his mom on the couch reading a book. "Studying?"

"I have to write a three page paper. It's due tomorrow."

"You'll do great."

Petunia looked up at Odo. "I almost forgot, your friend Ralph stopped by to make sure your dad's windshield was okay. Such a nice man, very polite."

A chill rolled through Odo. "What did he say?"

"He asked how you were doing, if you were staying out of trouble, not dropping any more bowling balls through car windows."

Albert snorted. "I think King Odo learned his lesson."

"Thanks. I'm going to run upstairs and do some homework."

Odo took a seat at his desk, drumming his fingers. Who was Ralph and what was he up to? He definitely wasn't just a friendly windshield repairman. Groceries aren't cheap, and he bought four bags of them for Harold. And why did he stop by the house and ask about the windshield?

Three hours later the sun had set, Odo's eyes drooping. "This homework is so boring. I learned all this math years ago, but I have to turn in my homework to get good grades so I can get into a good college. Only one more year." Odo frowned. "I wonder what Sephie is going to do after we graduate? She could go to any school she wanted to. I don't want the Odd Squad to break up if we all go to different schools."

Odo stood up, stepping across the room. He opened his dresser drawer, eyeing the gleaming medallion Nokk and Elia had given him. The good news was the medallions would let them visit each other no matter where they were going to school. He tucked the medallion inside a sock and hid it away in the drawer. He walked over to the window, peering out through the blinds to check the weather, a frown crossing his face when he saw the white van parked across the street, its motor running, parking lights on. He squinted, reading the shadowy letters on the side of the van.

Ralph's Windshield Repair Service
There in 15 minutes or the job is free!

"This is getting seriously creepy. I'm going to find out who Ralph is and what he wants."

Odo cracked his door open, peering down the hallway. The lights were off, his parents in bed. He crept down the stairs, easing open the front door and stepping outside, spotting a dark figure leaning against the van. He recognized the cowboy hat. It was Ralph.

Odo stepped across the street, his eyes on the silhouetted figure. "What are you doing here? Why did you give groceries to Harold? I know he's not your uncle."

Ralph stepped out of the shadows, the streetlight shining down on him, giving him an eerie spectral glow. "I like Harold and he needed groceries. What's wrong with that? Welcome back from Pangaea, by the way. I see you managed to get back without my help. I've been told that Varania is lovely this time of year."

"What? How do you know about that? What do you mean get back without your help?"

Ralph took off his hat and sunglasses.

Odo's jaw dropped. He took a step back, staring at Ralph "It's *you*!"

"Correct, it's me, Ralph the Windshield Repairman."

"You're Mike the Mechanic, I'd recognize you

anywhere."

"Mike the Mechanic? I fix windshields, not car engines."

"You know exactly who Mike the Mechanic is. We've talked to you on three different worlds. Does Charon the Ferryman ring any bells? Or Bakis Merriweather in Palusia?"

"Oh drat, you're far too clever for me, you tricked me into revealing my secret identity. You got me, I'm Mike the Mechanic and I fix leaky dihydrogen monoxide pipes."

Odo glared at him. "Don't even start that! Dihydrogen monoxide is water, and you're not a plumber. What are you doing here? How do you know Harold? Spill it, or else."

"Fine, I'll tell you everything. But first comes our traditional three question challenge. Get one answer correct and you can ask me any question you want."

"I'm not taking one of your ridiculous three question challenges. They're all trick questions and impossible to answer. Forget it."

"Your friend Sephie answered them correctly."

"Because you ask her ridiculously easy questions and you ask me impossibly hard ones. Something is really wrong with you. You're a very disturbed person."

"As you wish, no three question challenge. I'll be on my way then. Give my regards to Uncle Harold." Ralph turned, stepping toward the van door.

Odo groaned. "Fine, you win, I'll take your dumb three question challenge."

"Live and learn, as I always say."

Chapter 42

The Question

"You never say that, and you didn't tell me how you know about Pangaea and Varania. No one knows we went there. Wait, you said I managed to get back from Pangaea without your help. Did you bring me back the first time, when the molten volcanic rocks were falling from–"

"Do you want to take the three question challenge or not? Just answer one question correctly and you can ask me any question you want. Sound fair?"

Odo rolled his eyes. "It's never fair, your questions are ridiculous, like asking me to name all two thousand characters in Marcel Proust's *In Search of Lost Time* in thirty seconds."

"That was a tough one, I will admit that. I'll tell you what, I promise to give you a very easy question, one I know you'll absolutely be able to answer. How does that sound?"

"You always say that and then it's something crazy like what's *your* favorite kind of pie. How could I possibly have known what your favorite kind of pie is?"

"That was a trick question, I will admit that also. Not to worry, no trick questions this time. Easy peasy. Let me know when you're ready."

"Fine, I'm ready. Go ahead, ask your three questions."

"All right, here we go. Hold on, I'll tell you what, to make things even easier for you, this will be a one time only, one question challenge, not a three question challenge."

"That's not easier, it's harder. I only get one chance to answer correctly instead of three chances."

"You are a clever one, my mistake, I was never very good at statistics. Unfortunately, it's too late to change the rules back since they've already been changed once, and rules are rules, as I always say."

"You're not very good at logic either. You can't change the rules, then say you can't change the rules again because you already–"

"I have one question for you, and one question only, an easy yes or no question. Let me know when you're ready to answer the question. You have fifteen seconds left."

"I already said I was ready. Ask me the question."

"Do you love Sephie?"

Odo froze. "What?"

"It's a simple question, yes or no?"

Odo stared at Mike the Mechanic, his mind spinning, eyes wide. "What kind of question is that? That's personal, none of your business."

"You never said it couldn't be a personal question. Tick tock, time is running out. You have ten seconds left to answer. Do you love Sephie?"

"I think so. Maybe."

"I'm afraid the one question challenge requires a yes or no answer."

"Yes."

"Congratulations, you answered the question correctly and you've won the One Time Only, One Question Challenge. Well done, sir. You may now ask me any question you wish."

"What are you doing here?"

"I'm here to give you this." Mike the Mechanic reached into his coat pocket and pulled out a small white box tied with a green ribbon.

"What is it?"

"Oh, dear, I thought I had been crystal clear about the rules. You only get to ask one question. If you remember, I said you could ask me any question you wanted, singular, not plural. You had one question, and you asked me why I was here."

"That's not fair, I only get one question?"

"That's another question, I'm afraid."

"Fine, give me the present."

Mike the Mechanic handed the box to Odo. "This is a special gift for a truly remarkable person."

Odo eyed the gift suspiciously. "What is it?"

"Sorry, that's another question. It's time for me to go. Mr. Varania in apartment 2B has a leaky dihydrogen monoxide pipe that needs fixing."

"Something is so wrong with you."

Mike the Mechanic laughed as he climbed into his van.

Odo headed back to his house, gently closing the front door, creeping back up to his room. He flopped down on his bed, thinking about the question Mike the Mechanic had asked. Maybe it was true. Maybe he did love Sephie. Mike the Mechanic said he'd answered the question correctly.

He gazed at the white box curiously. "It's kind of weird that he's so mean to me but said I was a truly remarkable person. Maybe Sephie was right, maybe he's not such a bad guy."

Odo pulled the ribbon off, raising the lid, peering inside. "What is this?" He pulled out a second wrapped box, reading the gift tag.

For Professor Harold B. Livingstone

"It's not for me? It's for Harold?" Odo tossed the package onto his desk. "That guy is a total lunatic."

Odo took the gift to school the next day, showing it to the others at lunch.

"Why would Mike the Mechanic give you a gift for Harold?"

"Why does he do anything? He's a lunatic."

Sephie said, "Did he make you take one of his three question challenges?"

"Not exactly."

"Not exactly? Did he or didn't he?"

"He gave me a one time only one question challenge."

Silas said, "What was the question? Was it a crazy hard one?"

"It was hard, but I got it right. We should take this to Harold after school. What time do you want to go?"

Emmy said, "What was the question he asked?"

Odo shifted uncomfortably in his chair. "I don't know, it was kind of personal. I don't want to talk about it."

Silas gave a cackling laugh. "Spill it, Odo. What was the question?"

"I don't want to talk about it."

Sephie scanned his brainwaves, a smile flickering across her face. "You don't have to tell us if you don't want to. Let's all go to Harold's after school. I'm really curious about what Ralph's gift is."

Emmy said, "Maybe it's a dinosaur fossil or something. Or a dinosaur egg."

"That would be so cool. I'd love to have a pet dinosaur. A little pterosaur would be fun. It could fly around the house, maybe sit on my shoulder."

The bell rang, the four friends heading off to their classes, Sephie strolling along next to Odo. "You said Mike the Mechanic's question was a really hard one?"

Odo shrugged. "Not that hard, I guess."

"Hmm."

"What?"

"Nothing. You answered it correctly?"

"Mike the Mechanic said I did."

Sephie grinned. "See you after class."

The four friends met up after school, taking the bus home and heading down Asper Street to Harold's house.

"What do you think is in the box?"

"It's not very heavy, whatever it is."

Emmy said, "It's so mysterious. I wonder what kind of gift Mike the Mechanic would give someone?"

"It's probably one of those giant springy paper snakes that pops out and scares everyone."

Sephie knocked on the front door, waiting for it to open.

"Maybe he's taking a nap."

Odo twisted the knob. "It's not locked. I wish he wouldn't do that, it's not safe." He pushed the door open, calling out, "Harold? Are you home?"

"Maybe he's not here. Maybe he's walking to the moon or something."

Sephie was getting a bad feeling.

Chapter 43

Goodbyes

"Harold? Are you home?"

They stepped inside, walking down the hallway to the sitting room. Harold was sitting on the couch staring off into space.

"Harold? Are you okay?"

"Harold, it's me, Odo Whitley."

He turned slowly, looking at the four friends with a puzzled expression. "Hello. Are you here about the dinosaur? I think a dinosaur has been eating my food."

"We took him back to Varania. His name was Prince Nokk. Do you remember him?"

Harold shook his head. "I think there was a dinosaur in my house."

Odo took a seat next to him. "How are you feeling?"

"I'm hungry. I don't know when I ate."

Sephie said, "I'll make you a tuna sandwich. You like tuna."

"Excellent. I think I do like tuna."

Odo took Mike the Mechanic's gift from his pocket.

"I have a present for you. Someone I know wanted you to have this."

"My father used to give me presents."

"I know he did. He gave you nice presents."

Odo handed him the box.

Harold fumbled with the package, trying to untie the ribbon. "It's in a knot. It's confusing."

"I'll do it." Odo untied the ribbon, opening the box in front of Harold.

A big smile appeared on Harold's face. "My favorite, an oatmeal raisin cookie! This is my lucky day." He grabbed the cookie, taking a bite. "Delicious. I think my mother used to make oatmeal cookies for me when I was small. I don't know where my dad is. Delicious cookie. Very good."

Sephie stepped out of the kitchen with a tuna sandwich in her hand. "What was in the box?"

Odo said, "An oatmeal cookie. Why would Ralph give Harold an oatmeal cookie?"

"Because he likes them?"

Harold nodded. "I do like them. My lucky day." He blinked, opening and closing his mouth. "I feel strange. I think something is wrong with my–" Before Odo could react, Harold slumped over onto the couch, his eyes closed.

Emmy gave a shriek. "What happened? What's wrong with him?"

"Odo, call the paramedics. I think he's sick. Maybe

there was something in the cookie."

"Mike the Mechanic poisoned him?"

"Call the paramedics. Now!"

Odo was grabbing for his phone when Harold abruptly sat up. "What happened? Where am I? What are you doing here?"

"I'm Odo Whitley. Do you remember me?"

"Of course I do. What I don't know is where I've been and why you're in my house."

The four friends gaped at Harold. "You remember who we are?"

"You're the Odd Squad; Odo, Sephie, Silas, and Emmy. Where's Prince Nokk?"

"You're feeling okay?"

"I feel like I just woke up. Have I been sleeping?"

"You were having a hard time remembering things."

"What was in that cookie? Where did you get it?"

"Cookie?"

"The oatmeal raisin cookie you gave me. Where did you get it?"

"Someone gave it to me?"

"Who?"

"It's a little complicated, but his name is Mike the Mechanic."

"That explains it."

"Do you know him?"

"Everyone knows him. Where's Prince Nokk?"

"He's back in Varania. He's the emperor now. He

turned out to be really nice."

"I thought he was from Pangaea?"

"He was hiding there because people on Varania found out he was a genetically altered mutant and wanted to kill him. He can warp space and send people through temporal wormholes into the future."

"Hmm. Interesting."

"How do you know Mike the Mechanic?"

"I met him in my travels."

"Using the medallion?"

Harold nodded. "I've done a lot of traveling, met a lot of people."

"What do you think was in the cookie he gave you?"

Harold shrugged. "Something that healed me, nano-bots or something similar."

"Why do you think he did it? Why did Mike the Mechanic heal you?"

"There's only one person who knows why Mike the Mechanic does the things he does, and that's Mike the Mechanic. All I know is he saved my life. I didn't have much time left. I'm not afraid of dying, I just don't want to go yet."

Odo was remembering their recent adventures with Charon the Ferryman in the Land of the Almost Dead.

Emmy said, "What are you going to do now? Will you start teaching paleontology again?"

"I'm going to take a nice long vacation."

"That sounds fun. Where will you go?"

"Pangaea. This time I'm taking cameras, recording what I see. I have some friends there who will set me up with some very high tech equipment to keep me safe."

"How long will you be gone?"

Harold hesitated, then said, "I don't think I'll be coming back."

"You're not coming back? How come?"

"I've been here long enough. It's time to move on. I'll donate my collection to the Natural History Museum. You're welcome to take a few things if you see anything you'd like."

"Really?"

"I owe you my life. If it wasn't for the four of you… well, you know."

Odo strolled around the room, studying the fossils and artifacts. "This is all so amazing. It really does belong in a museum so people can see it. What's that giant tooth?"

"That's a real T-rex tooth, not a fossil. It holds the complete DNA sequence of the T-rex, in case you want to clone one. It's yours if you want it."

"Really? It's incredible. I'm pretty sure cloning one would be a really bad idea."

Sephie said, "Don't even think about it."

"Silas, how about this T-rex claw?"

"I'd love it! It's huge. Thank you."

Sephie and Emmy had each picked out a pterosaur fossil when Harold said, "Oh, I almost forgot." He stepped over to a box on a top shelf, pulling out four rocks. "Moon rocks, one for each of you. They're worth a fortune, but it's illegal to sell them. I picked them up on one of my walks."

Sephie said, "I wish you didn't have to go. It's so much fun to visit you. We're going to miss you."

Odo nodded. "A lot."

"And I will miss you also. I always say that life is a long series of goodbyes, but there are also a lot of marvelous hellos. If you have more hellos than goodbyes, you're doing well."

The moving van arrived at Harold's house four days later.

Chapter 44

The Queen's Gift

Sephie called Odo when she found the silver box tucked away in her backpack.

"You didn't open it without us did you?"

"Of course not, we can open it at your house."

Odo said, "The queen said she hoped it would bring us happiness. What do you think she meant?"

"Maybe it's a holographic game console with five hundred cool games."

"Did she say something about that?"

Sephie laughed. "She didn't tell me anything. It's a little silver box. Whatever it is, it's small, no more than five or six inches long."

"How soon can you come over?"

"We'll be there in an hour. I already called Silas and Emmy. Try not to go crazy wondering what it is."

"Too late."

Sephie laughed. "See you soon."

Silas, Emmy, and Odo were waiting for Sephie on the front steps when she arrived. She took a seat next to them, pulling the box from her coat pocket.

"Open it!"

"Not so fast, Odo. How about we each guess what it is? Whoever is closest gets a free ticket and candy at the next movie we go to."

Odo groaned. "This is torture. Okay, I say it's a weird alien insect who tells nonstop hilarious jokes."

"The queen said it would make us happy, not drive us crazy."

"What's that supposed to mean? What's wrong with jokes?"

Silas said, "I think it's an ancient mystical relic that will grant all our wishes."

"Good one."

Emmy said, "I think it's a tiny elephant that sings beautiful romantic ballads while it strums a dulcimer."

Odo and Silas stared at her. "What?"

Sephie said, "I think it's a picture of Odo."

Silas leaned over, pretending to barf. "Gaggh!"

Odo grinned. "Thanks, Sephie."

Sephie set the box on her lap, her finger on the latch. "Ready?"

"Yes, we're ready, open it!"

She flipped the lid open.

Odo stared silently at the box.

Silas said, "It's a feather."

"A green feather."

"Nobody wins the prize. We weren't even close."

"Why would she give us a green feather?"

Silas said, "Maybe we're supposed to tickle each other with it? That would sort of make you happy. We'd be laughing and stuff."

"You're so deranged."

Sephie studied the four-inch long green feather. "It's just a plain green feather. How could it bring us happiness?"

Odo shrugged. "I guess if you had a huge feather collection, and the only feather you were missing was one from a rare green–" He stopped short, letting out a yelp. "I know what it is!"

"What is it?"

"It's not just a feather, it's something else."

"What?"

"It's a waystone."

Sephie gasped, "The bright green bird in our beach dream!"

"Bingo. This must be a waystone that will take us to that beach. It wasn't a dream, it was a real place. We traveled to a real world in our dream, and this feather is from the bird I saw running along the shore."

"Touch it. If it makes your finger tingle, it's a waystone."

Odo touched the feather, jerking his finger back. "It's a waystone, and a powerful one."

The following Saturday, the Odd Squad set off for the movie theater but never arrived. They were halfway there when they stepped into a side alley, Odo using the green feather to shift them to a pristine white sandy beach, waves rolling onto the shore, tall palm trees swaying gently in a warm breeze.

Silas ran down to the shore, dipping his toes in the water. "It's perfect, not cold at all. This is amazing."

"There's a shed over there, let's check it out." Odo darted over to the shed, pulling the wooden door open.

"No way! Beach chairs and surfboards! Where did they come from? Do you think the queen put them here?"

"Who else could it be? She gave us the feather."

They dragged the beach chairs out of the shack, setting them on the sand.

"They're just like the ones in my dream, the same green and white stripes." Odo looked around, saying, "I think we were sitting right about here in our dream, right near those two palm trees."

Emmy jumped up when she spotted the big spider racing down the beach toward them. She squinted, giving a shout. "It's Plato!"

"No way! What's he doing here?" They waved to him as he drew closer.

Plato stopped in front of them, saying, "You did it, you figured out what the green feather was for! We thought it would be fun for you because you love solving mysteries. How do you like your island?"

"This is ours?"

"The queen has decreed it. It's yours forever."

"Our own private island! How cool is that?"

"Plato, how did you get here?"

"I live here, this is Argonia."

"Sephie and I had a dream we were here, sitting in beach chairs exactly like these."

"The chairs and the floating boards are from Elia and Emperor Nokk. He said he saw pictures of the floating boards on your world and thought you'd like them."

"The floating boards are called surfboards, and they're super fun."

"Plato, do you live on this island?"

"I live three islands north of here, about twelve miles from this one. The planet is covered with millions of small islands, but most of Argonia's surface is water."

Odo said, "So, just curious about what kinds of creatures live in the ocean here?"

"There are lots of plants and about a million kinds of little fish, nothing scary."

"Excellent, no giant hungry pliosaurs." Odo eyed the long rolling waves breaking onto the beach. "Who wants to try surfing?"

Silas jumped up and grabbed a surfboard. "Cowabunga!"

Emmy laughed. "Don't forget, I used to be one of the cool kids in my alternate timeline."

"You know how to surf?"

"Watch and learn, bro."

"Don't ever call me that again."

Odo said, "Hey, Plato, do you want to try surfing?"

"I don't need a floating board. Argonians float, riding the currents from one island to another. That's how we evolved, how our species spread across the planet."

"You just jump in the water and float?"

Plato ran down to the shoreline, leaping into the water, floating like a huge furry beach ball, paddling around with his eight long legs. "Sometimes we just let the wind carry us wherever it will. It's quite relaxing."

Odo grabbed his surfboard, carrying it down to the water's edge. Emmy hopped onto her board, paddling out a few hundred feet, waiting for a wave. A few minutes later she caught one, standing up and riding it all the way to the shore, zig zagging back and forth across the cresting wave.

"No way! Did you see that?"

Three hours later the friends carried their boards back to the shed. "That was so fun. I'm exhausted."

Odo said, "Let's vote on who's the second best surfer."

"This isn't a surfing championship, Odo. Not everything is a competition. We're here to relax and have fun. Is anyone hungry? I can shape us some lunch. How about pizza?"

Odo was finishing his third slice of pizza when he heard screeching laughter. Silas had been unsuccessfully attempting a cartwheel through a wave, doing a calamitous face plant in the water, Emmy laughing hysterically.

As he watched Silas and Emmy laughing, Odo realized how much each of them had changed since he'd met them. They were so different now, so much happier. He also realized how much he and Sephie had changed since they met Silas and Emmy. It was almost magical, their friendship like water and sunlight on a garden. Sephie was right, gold coins were nothing, friendship was everything. He glanced over at her, remembering Mike the Mechanic's question.

Odo Whitley leaned back in his green and yellow striped canvas beach chair, gazing across the pristine white sandy beach, a pair of nearby palm trees swaying gently in the ocean breeze. A green bird with long yellow legs was racing along the shoreline, scouting the area for its next meal.

If you enjoyed reading

The Translucent Boy and the
Man Who Walked to the Moon

please leave a short review or rating
on Amazon.com
Reviews are the lifeblood of indie publishers –
we can't survive without them!

If you have any comments or suggestions
or would like to be notified of upcoming book
releases and Free Kindle book day promotions,
please email me at
OrvilleMouse@gmail.com

Follow me at:
www.facebook.com/TomHoffmanAuthor/

Best wishes until we meet again,

Tom Hoffman

ABOUT THE AUTHOR

Tom Hoffman received a B.S. in psychology
from Georgetown University in 1972
and a B.A. in 1980 from the now-defunct
Oregon College of Art. He has lived in Alaska
with his wife since 1973. They have two
adult children and three adorable
grandchildren. Tom was a graphic designer
and artist for over 35 years.
Redirecting his imagination from art to
writing, he wrote his first novel,
The Eleventh Ring, at age 63.